MANA
(and other gifts from heaven.)
And then, God Sent His Son.

By

Bill Daly

Scripture taken from the Holy Bible, New International Version ®. NIV ®. Copyright © 1973, 1978, 1984 by International Bible Society. Used by permission of Zondervan Publishing House. All rights reserved.

Scripture taken from the Apocryphal Gospels. Translation copyright © Simon Gathercole, 2021

Mana
(What is it?)

Mana came down from heaven as a gift of God's love for His people. God's Son came down from heaven as a gift of His love for all of the world.

After Moses led the Israelites out of Egypt, the people grumbled for they missed their old lives where they had no hunger and no worries as to where their next meal was to come from. In the wilderness after their escape from Egypt they had nothing to eat. God heard the cries of His people and responded.

Everyday God supplied his people with a bread-like food called Mana in the morning, and quail in the evening for forty years. Even in our own lives today, God continues to provide His people with gifts from heaven to remind us of His unending love for each of us.

From the time of Moses to our current days, God's people continue to be self-focused and complain and continue to sin against Him. And yet, even still, He continues to shower us with his blessings and His comforting grace.

In Hebrew, mana translates to "what is it?" It saved the Israelites yet they knew not what it was. And they grumbled. In another time God sent His only begotten Son to save an ungrateful and sinful world. Mana, again. And the world knew Him not - so instead they crucified Him.

Author's Comments

This is a book of fiction. A Biblical novel. Some of the character names you will recognize are a part of Biblical history, while others are my own creation. The words spoken by Jesus come directly from the Bible and I would never create words not spoken by Him in this story, nor would I use them out of context.

Much of the story line is based upon a blend of truth, of facts, legend, and conjecture. Personally, I found it interesting that my characters and topic research lead me to a new understanding about the life and times during the days of living with Jesus. I hope that you too will discover an interest in finding new things that envelope life in the first century.

Why did I write this book? I love the Bible, and the Word! But we all know that for every Scripture verse there is always a "back story" of what led up to that moment in Scripture. I have created these fictitious characters and moments to weave together a story that hopefully may ignite a passion within your own spirit and encourage you to spend more time with the person of Jesus Christ and His Word.

The Bible is ALIVE. It is God's Word and His Word is just as relevant today as it was when He created the world. I know that each of us needs to be reminded that the Bible is not a bookend nor a coffee table decoration. It is *HOW* God speaks to us today. It is truly a piece of intricate art where the mysteries are revealed, the pieces come together through Old Testament prophesy and the deliverance of prophesy fulfilled in the New Testament. Yet the story does not end there at all.

My prayer for you is that if this fictitious story can bring you closer to initiating an interest in reading the Bible, and beginning a personal relationship with Jesus Christ, then I have succeeded. If this happens to you? Then Hallelujah! God's plan, not mine.

For Beverly, the love of my life.

MANA

"Then the Lord said to Moses, 'I will rain down bread from heaven for you. The people are to go out each day and gather enough for that day. In this way I will test them and see whether they will follow my instructions. On the sixth day they are to prepare what they bring in, and that is to be twice as much as they gather on the other days.'" (Exodus 16:4-5)

"When the magi had departed, an angel from the Lord appeared to Joseph in a dream and said, "Get up. Take the child and his mother and escape to Egypt. Stay there until I tell you, for Herod will soon search for the child in order to kill him." Joseph got up and, during the night, took the child and his mother to Egypt."
(Matthew 2: 13-14)

Gestas
(To complain)

I heard them coming more than I saw them. A donkey pulling a cart. But it was more than that. It sounded like a lamb crying but not exactly. What is that sound anyway?

From where I was hiding, I didn't want to risk them seeing me. This was my favorite hiding spot for my ambushes. The passageway is called Via Maris which is the well-traveled route that most take on their way to Egypt. The sand and gravel has been compacted by thousands of travelers over hundreds of years. It also offers many twists and turns over an undulating surface along with occasional rock and boulder beds. My favorite spot is just after a lazy turn, and has several large boulders to hide amongst. It is a good spot. I am hidden well.

It has been a good week already. My attacks have been efficient and profitable. Indeed! It has been a good week with the treasure I have secured. My attack method of ambush is fast and efficient. The strategy is always the same. When I emerge from my hiding spot, I run towards them while brandishing my large wooden mallet, mostly startling them by my sudden appearance, and then they are frozen and stunned and fearful. I will see panic painted on their faces, to which I actually enjoy. I feel the power that I have over them. They see the intensity in my eyes and they become frozen. I begin screaming at them driving them further into their immediate fear. I will strike in just a few more moments.

I hear the cart approaching and now it is only a matter of time before I begin my assault. What is that crying sound? No, not a lamb, it sounds more human. Oh wait. No, not a lamb, but a baby crying! Yes. The sound is a baby crying! It's time for my assault; time to move. Move, move, move. Now! Attack!

The pathway that I'm located on splits the surrounding cavernous rock bed. There are many hiding places on each side of this section of the pathway, but this is my favorite. Large rocks, more like boulders, provide a great cover for my assaults. Surprise is my ally. It's time now! Move quickly now! I jump into the path of the passing cart. And everything happens very quickly!

Usually, as I land in front of the cart, the travelers are startled and taken by surprise. For even a greater effect, I swing my large wooden club and scream for them to stop, which they always do. Then, while still wondering where I came from, I usually hit the cart with my club and order everyone off the cart and corral the travelers together. This way I contain any forceful attempted resistance from them and, if they decide to resist, I can easily strike at least one of them with enough force that they quickly surrender. They are too surprised by my attack to even think about defending themselves. I then steal the valuable items that I am able to carry away, and escape running up the boulder path up into the hills. No one ever chases me. They are just happy to be left unharmed.

Oh, that's not to say that some have tried to resist or fight back! Some think that they will win against me and my club. None have won or beaten me yet. If I am attacked, I usually swing my heavy club low. They don't expect that. They think my first parry will be high and prepare themselves defensively waiting for my move. No, I swing for their legs, usually right around the knees. Surprise is my friend, again. So far, I have only had to kill twice. I didn't like doing it but I must be victorious with my quest. Their treasure is mine!

I make my move and jump in front of this cart. A woman holding a baby is startled and screams immediately. She screams, and the baby goes from crying to screaming. I believe the baby senses the mother's fear. There is fear in the air. I am pleased. The noise only compliments their fear.

Next, I see what I guess would be the father of the screaming baby, and he had been walking, leading the donkey who was pulling the cart. He is now directly in front of me. He is startled and stops the donkey's progress, and jumps back slightly as he is taken by total surprise as well. I am swinging my club in a circular fashion above my head while I am yelling telling them to stop exactly where they are. They do. I ask them what goods are they transporting in their cart and where is their money. The money is always the fastest thing to escape with.

The man cries out "please, please don't hurt us. We are just trying to get to Egypt! We need to get there for our own safety. Please we have nothing to offer you. It's just my wife Mary, and our son Jesus. Please spare us!" I am still swinging my club over my head and am ready to hit the wooden cart with my heavy club. This man, the father of this baby, suddenly drops to his knees into a prayer-like position saying "please, please, please".

I hit the side of the cart with my club, splintering the wooden side of it.

I never saw what happened next.

Talia
(Dew from God)

It was a normal day for me. I was in my thirteenth year and I was doing my normal morning chores at the synagogue here in Galilee. Jairus, my father, is the leader of our synagogue. Everyday, I clean the inside of the synagogue which includes dusting the embroidered Torah Binders, the Torah mantle, and the curtains of the Holy Ark. I really don't mind this work because it is easy work, and I am very happy to take care of the Lord's Temple. It makes me happy to think I am helping to serve our powerful God.

This morning my father rose early and left our house even before my mother and I awoke. This was something he never did. He did tell mother and I that he would be leaving just after sunrise in order to reach Bethany before the heat of the day arose. He seemed to be very anxious and told us he wanted to meet this man they called Rabbi. His real name was Jesus. He was from a smaller town called Nazareth. The word of his healing powers was traveling quickly throughout our land and my father spoke of him and the things that he was doing with great joy and curiosity.

Of course I too am curious about this man named Jesus and I cannot wait to see my father again to hear about what he discovers about this man. I have heard that people crowd him so much that he can hardly even move forward. Crowds that only a King would see. Amazing.

But right now? I'm thinking of Noam, my friend Noam. The one who teases me about how long my hair is and that I have such skinny arms. I don't like that part, but then he will say to me "your eyes are the most beautiful I have ever seen" or even sometimes he will say "your smile just melts my heart". When he says things like that? Something happens to me. I don't know exactly how to describe it, but I feel flush, hot in the face. I feel nervous but feel excited. And then he smiles at me. Oh my. I love to see his face and how he looks at me.

"Talia! Where are you? You need to come to the well with me! Where are you girl?"

My Mom should know that I'm in the Temple! What's with her? She knows this is my "every morning".

"Mother, I am almost finished dusting the Torah Binders and I am almost finished with my all of my chores! I will be with you shortly!"

"Well hurry now child", says mother, "today is going to be a very hot day and we need to get to the well very soon.". Mothers! They always have something for us to do.

I wonder where Noam is today? I'm smiling because my mind has placed this handsome boy right in front of me. Such a warm feeling it gives me!

"Ok, mother, I'm coming!"

Noam
(Tenderness)

"In the fifteenth year of the rule of the emperor Tiberius - when Pontius Pilate was governor over Judea and Herod was ruler over Galilee, his brother Phillip was ruler over Ituraea and Trachonitas, and Lysanais was ruler over Abilene, during the high priesthood of Annas and Caiaphas – God's word came to John son of Zecharia in the wilderness. John went throughout the region of the Jordan River, calling for people to be baptized to show that they were changing their hearts and lives and wanted God to forgive their sins. This is just as it was written in the scroll of the words of Isaiah the prophet, A voice crying out in the wilderness: 'Prepare the way for the Lord; make his paths straight. Every valley will be filled, and every mountain and hill will be leveled. The crooked will be made straight and the rough places made smooth. All humanity will see God's salvation.'" (Luke 3:1-20)

Man I am hot. The sun is high now and the air is dry. This line I am standing in appears to go on forever! No kidding. It does move ahead, but ever so slowly. I even arrived early this morning yet the line was already long. We are all waiting our turn. From the things I have heard, this man John, is a true healer. It's easy for all of us to know that our land needs healing! There is so much anguish among the people that it is hard to be hopeful. The Roman's have made things very hard for us, and even our own Rome appointed rulers, and the Temple leaders, and the tax collectors, and the moneychangers, are all corrupt. There is little trust among the people and many are desperate. We need hope. I need hope! I am only 15 years old and I feel like I need to be excited about the life ahead of me instead of this feeling of dread. I need a change in my life. That's why I am standing in this line. I need a new beginning.

I believe this is the fourth day that this strange man has been in this section of the Jordan River. At first, most of the crowds were commoners, just people of the land. Farmers, bakers, shepherds. Now I've been told that more and more people are arriving from positions of respect within our community. Some just stand and watch, while others are participating and being baptized. Me? I feel like this baptism-thing will cleanse me, and bring into me a new spirit that will guide me with my future. As I shuffle along in this line, I am finally getting close enough in position to John and I am feeling the excitement from those who are coming out of the river. They are calling him John the Baptist. I'm now getting close enough that I can hear him; hear him blessing those he is baptizing.

"Hey there, move out of my way young man", as he pushes me back while he takes over my position in line. The man is big and much stronger than I. "Yes sir. Please. Yes, please take my place in line. Thank you for allowing me to let you in."

This is what I mean. People do not respect one another and those who are strong and powerful, simply take what they want from us. Someday, maybe I too will have respect from others and they will respect me. I need a break in my fortune. I keep hearing this word, repent. People are praying as they are getting closer to their baptism, and I hear their confessions of repentance. Change your ways. Repent.

I remember my father saying that a lot. "People need to repent son" he'd say. "They are always looking out for them selves." My father worked down at the Temple stables and he was in charge of cleaning them out. It was an endless job and not a very nice job to have but at least he had a job. I know he worked hard, because I never saw him after I awoke in the mornings and never in the evenings before I went to bed. My mother would always tell us kids, "your father works so hard for what we have". What *do* we have? I have nothing. We still have nothing. I need hope in my life. I am hoping that by being baptized I will begin anew; a fresh start.

My goodness, the time has come! I'm next! I'm next in line! I can see him now very clearly. Yes, he is dressed in sackcloth, just as I have been told. My father has told me that when men adorn sackcloth it means they are in mourning or they want to show of a repentance for sin.

"Do you see that, young man?" says the man standing behind me. "He wears a garment of camel's hair and has a leather girdle around his waist; the same as the prophet Elijah did. It has been written in the book of Malachi foretelling: "*See, I will send you the prophet Elijah before that great and dreadful day of the Lord comes. He will turn the hearts of the fathers to their children, and the hearts of the children to their fathers; or else I will come and strike the land with a curse.*" (Malachi 4:5).

"You see, my brother?" he continues. "We are being shown a sign that the Lord is coming! Yes that's right. Yes sir. Just as Malachi has told us. A King will come not only to judge his people, but also to bless and restore them! I believe this is the fulfillment of Malachi's prophesy – the Lord has come! You see? This is why John is dressed so – the Lord has come! It is time to repent before it is too late!"

"Then John said to the crowds who came to be baptized by him, 'You children of snakes! Who warned you to escape from the angry judgment that is coming soon? Produce fruit that shows you have changed your hearts and lives.' The crowds asked him, 'What then should we do?' He answered, 'Whoever has two shirts must share with the one who has none, and whoever has food must do the same.'

Even tax collectors came to be baptized. They said to him, 'Teacher, what should we do?' He replied, 'Collect no more than you are authorized to collect.' Soldiers asked, 'What about us? What should we do?' He answered, 'Don't cheat or harass anyone and be satisfied with your pay.'

The people were filled with expectation and everyone wondered whether John might be the Christ. (Luke 3:1-20)

Those sent by the Pharisees asked ' Why do you baptize if you aren't the Christ, nor Elijah, nor the prophet?' (John 1: 24-25) *John replied to them all, 'I baptize you with water, but the one who is more powerful than me is coming. I'm not worthy to loosen the strap of his sandals. He will baptize you with the Holy Spirit and fire.' (Luke 3:15-16)*

I stood at the river's edge waiting for John to call me to him. I must admit, I am nervous but I feel a calm inside. I can't explain it but that's the way I feel. "Come to me my friend" John says to me. He then took me into his arms, said a blessing over me and dunked me into the river. And there it was. I am baptized! I'm not sure exactly how I feel, but I do feel different! Somehow, in that instant, my heart has been opened and I feel differently; I'm not sure why or how to describe it. I do feel a sense of hope again. I feel a sense of peace within my soul. It's such a feeling that must sit right down now and adjust my senses. Almost like I could faint!

As I look around, heading back to the shoreline, I see a small group of men huddled under a nearby tree. They too look like their lives have changed in some way that they too are adjusting to. I walk over to join their huddle.

"Welcome brother" is their greeting to me. "Join us here; come, sit." As I settled down to take a seat on the grass, one of them asked me "we have heard that He will be here soon; the one named Jesus. Have you seen him?"

Before I could answer, all of a sudden there was a great commotion at the river's edge. There was John and he was spreading his arms out across his body in greeting to a new person. John looked as though this was no stranger to him however. I could see him with a broad smile on his face welcoming this man.

John cried out "*I need to be baptized by you, yet you come to me?*" (Matthew 3:14) This man, this must be Jesus!

Our group hurriedly rose to our feet and we ran over to be close to the river's edge and actually see this man named Jesus!

And Jesus spoke *"Allow me to be baptized now. This is necessary to fulfill all righteousness." So John agreed to baptize Jesus. When Jesus was baptized, he immediately came up out of the water. Heaven was opened to him, and he saw the spirit of God coming down like a dove and resting on him."* (Matthew 3:15-16)

We stood in awe of this moment. Something was in the air, just a different feeling and I felt it deep inside me. Not one of us spoke as we all felt it too. Silence surrounded all of us.

And then *"A voice from heaven said, 'This is my son whom I dearly love; I find happiness in him.'"* (Matthew 3:17) *"Even I didn't recognize him, but the one who sent me to baptize with water said to me, 'The one on whom you see the Spirit coming down and resting is the one who baptizes with the Holy Spirit'. I have seen and testified that this one is God's Son."* (John 1:33-34)

All of us fell to our knees! We all bowed our heads to touch the ground in this miraculous moment. Wait until I tell Talia of what happened here today. I must go now! This day was unbelievable!

I was saying good-bye to my new found friends, especially the one named Nathaniel. We really connected in our thoughts and attitudes towards John and our baptisms. We talked about our hopes of a Messiah that may be in our midst. So we pledged that we would meet again, and then I began my walk home. What exciting times I am living in!

Jacob
(May God Protect)

What's an old man to do? My son, Joseph has been a wonderful father, a very good businessman, a skilled craftsman, and he and his wife Mary have made me a proud grandfather to their children. But their oldest, Jesus, he has a mind of his own! He is very smart, with a strong tongue and has mastered the teachings of the Torah. The way he spends his days, with the elders, the Rabbis, and the leaders of the synagogue is so encouraging. He teaches as well as learns from his elders and he is very admired by all. I am very proud of him but now he has left us; he has left Nazareth on some type of mission he said. I tried to convince him to stay but he would have none of it.

Jesus was always a good boy, but he also had such an independent streak in him as well. Even as a young boy, he appeared to be led by a different spirit than most of the children his age. I remember that time when he was only twelve and it was the time of year when we celebrated the Jewish Passover Festival.

"Each year his parent's went to Jerusalem for the Passover Festival. When he was twelve years old, they went up to Jerusalem according to their custom. After the festival was over, they were returning home, but the boy Jesus stayed behind in Jerusalem. His parents didn't know it. Supposing that he was among their band of travelers, they journeyed on for a full day while looking for him among their family and friends. When they didn't find Jesus, they returned to Jerusalem to look for him. After three days they found him in the Temple. He was sitting among the teachers, listening to them, and putting questions to them. Everyone who heard him was amazed by his understanding and his answers. When his parents saw him, they were shocked.

His mother said, 'Child, why have you treated us like this? Listen! Your father and I have been worried. We have been looking for you!'

Jesus replied, 'Why were you looking for me? Didn't you know that is was necessary for me to be in my Father's house?' But they didn't understand what he said to them.

Jesus went down to Nazareth with them and was obedient to them. His mother cherished word in her heart. Jesus matured in wisdom and years, and in favor with God and with people." (Luke 2: 41-52)

Yes, Jesus is a good boy. Listen to me though? He is no longer a boy but a young man! And our townspeople love him. He is so gentle and always willing to help others. Especially the children! He loves their energy and vigor for life. He once told me that the reason why he loves the children so much is because they are not afraid. They love everyone and want to help others as best they can and they bear no discrimination. They treat everyone as equals. Yes, that is so true! When do they grow out of that?

He left several days ago now for Capernaum. Already I miss him so. But what can an old man do? Follow him around while he transverses all over this world? I no longer have that source of energy to be moving constantly and visiting so many. I will talk to Joseph and his mother and maybe they could give me some ideas on how I can follow his path. But I hate to burden poor Joseph. He looks so tired lately. His business is good but it is also stressful and easily wears down a man. So, I'm just sitting here wondering, what should I do?

The Prophesy
Isaiah 30:8-18

"Go now, write it on a tablet for them, inscribe it on a scroll, that for the days to come it may be an everlasting witness.

For these are rebellious people, deceitful children, children unwilling to listen to the Lord's instruction. They say to the seers, "See no more visions!" and to the prophets, "Give us no more visions of what is right! Tell us pleasant things, prophesy illusions. Leave this way, get off this path, and stop confronting us with the Holy One of Israel!"

Therefore this is what the Holy One of Israel says: "Because you have rejected this message, relied on oppression and depended on deceit, this sin will become for you like a high wall, cracked and bulging, that collapses suddenly, in an instant. It will break in pieces like pottery, shattered so mercilessly that among its pieces not a fragment will be found for taking coals from a hearth or scooping water out of a cistern."

This is what the Sovereign Lord, the Holy One of Israel, says: "In repentance and rest is your salvation, in quietness and trust is your strength, but you would have none of it. You said, 'No, we will flee on horses.' Therefore you will flee! You said, 'We will ride off on swift horses.' Therefore your pursuers will be swift! A thousand will flee at the threat of one; at the threat of five you will all flee away, till you are left like a flagstaff on a mountaintop, like a banner on a hill."

The Promise of God's Grace to Israel
Yet the Lord longs to be gracious to you; therefore he will rise up to show you compassion. For the Lord is a God of justice. Blessed are all who wait for him!"

Even in the time of Isaiah, the Jewish people preferred the darkness, and they really did not like to hear the Holy commandments and God's hatred of sin and they thought that they were wiser than the God they worshipped. The reality was only those who truly believed and were confident that God was the way, were the ones who had comfort.

The Lord waits patiently for us to come to Him so that He can take us under His wing, show us His love for us and His unending, undeserving compassion for us. Blessed are those who wait for His help.

The Jewish people were going through the proper rituals as told by God himself, but their hearts simply were not in them. They were corrupt spiritually, as well as morally. The coming of Jesus was a direct threat to their lifestyle and the religious leaders were threatened by this Rabi, this teacher, by His miracles, and His healings. Even through all of this, the people were hardened to the truth of Jesus. And if he was the Messiah? He was not establishing the kingdom of what the people were looking for – A king that would clear their lands and cast out the occupiers! No, this was Jesus, who came to give His life as a sacrifice for our sins and introduce His people to His Kingdom in heaven.

It has now been over 400 years since Isaiah foretold of His coming (and of His rejection) and the people have lost sight of God's purpose for us. There is hope for a Messiah, for a Savior, but we have waited so long and our faith is fractured. Where is God? Is there really a God? We should not suffer as we do if there really is a God!

Gestas
(To complain)

The Passover. What a time it is in Jerusalem! The crowds are everywhere jamming the streets where everyone struggles against the hoards of bodies, the street vendors, and the money changers at the Temple. So many people in one crowded city. The census-counters estimate that over 300,000 – 400,000 people have come to celebrate this annual festival. It is their custom; it is my good fortune. So many opportunities to pick pockets! This is my time of year! I love this time of the year!

As I make my way to the Temple, I am still in wonder at the throngs of people on the streets. Most of them look at me in disgust as they recognize me as one of the moneychangers. On my walk, the smell of smoked meats, and porridge fills my senses, the cries of the street merchants calling people to their displays as we all shuffle along. Every room within the city is filled with guests and travelers coming for the Passover. The stalls are filled with horses and donkeys that have pulled the carts to get them all here for the festival. It truly is a sight to see.

Yes, and those cheating merchants selling livestock and doves to those who needed to atone for their sins by making a perfect sacrifice at the Temple. These merchants were to be selling "perfect" animals according to the Jewish faith, except they were far from "perfect". Most, if not all, were all flawed in some way yet they represented them as "perfect in every way". Most of the pilgrims coming to the Passover are poor and cannot afford these prices but that's where I can help them. I have made a good business and provide these people with loans so they can afford to purchase a dove for their sacrifice to their God at the Temple.

None of this would have been possible if I hadn't met Flavius Obed, a very rich merchant indeed. Actually, I helped him fight off another scoundrel (like me) during an attempted robbery. You see, on one particular day, Flavius was on his way to deposit his business investment proceeds (his money) to the Temple bank when I spotted a thief hiding in a darkened doorway awaiting for Flavius to walk by. (Actually, I was positioning my own self to also attack Flavius that day.) However, as devious as I am, I decided to wait and see how things progressed with the other thief's attack.

As Flavius walked by the hidden thief, the thief jumped into his path and attempted to grab Flavius's satchel. As Flavius and the thief struggled, I ran into the tussle and struck the thief over the head with my club knocking him unconscious. I then grabbed Flavius and we ran down the alley fleeing to a more public street. "keep running with me, follow me" I said to him. When we reached the street corner, I slowed and we resumed into a normal walking pace. "Are you ok, sir?" I asked.

"Yes, yes. A little out of breath but I am fine. Thank you, thank you, for rescuing me from that bandit! I was totally defenseless and you saved me from who knows what! Why don't you join me at that shop ahead and I will buy us some tea."

"Well, of course sir." I replied. "That would be very nice of you." It was only a few more steps before we entered into the crowded café, found a table and ordered our tea.

"I am so grateful to you – what is your name my friend?"

"I am called Gestas" I replied. "Really, it is not a problem at all. I suppose I was just lucky enough to be there when you needed assistance. I am happy to help you Mr. ?"

"Ah yes, of course" he replied. "Well, I am nevertheless grateful for my luck then! Thank you. My name is Flavius Obed. My business is not too far from here and I was on my way to make a deposit at the Temple. Your timing was perfect and you saved me a lot of money today! Maybe even my life!"

"Mr. Obed, may I ask, why is it that you store your money at the Temple?"

"Oh my Mr. Gestas, can I call you Gestas?"

"Of course, of course, yes you may." I replied.

"Well, you see, I earn interest on the monies I keep at the Temple. The Rabbani at the Temple issue loans from the deposits like mine, to the moneychangers who in turn charge festival pilgrims for their loan services. The moneychangers charge a fee to the pilgrims so that they can exchange their Roman coins into the only coins that are accepted at the Temple; the Tyrian Shekel. The Tyrian Shekel is the only coin accepted because it has more silver than the Roman coin."

This was all fascinating to me. People like Mr. Obed earn interest by depositing their money into the Temple's treasury. The Temple makes money by granting loans to the moneychangers. The moneychangers make money by issuing loans to the pilgrims. Everyone in this exchange, except for the pilgrims, makes money! What a scheme it is. And if the pilgrim's loan is not repaid, the moneychanger has claim to their properties, or live stock, or any other assets that would cover the repayment of the loan. What a business. So now I am thinking "how" do I get into such a business as this? Right at that moment, I see Mr. Obed take his final swallow of tea and he begins to rise from our table.

"Well, Gestas, I must be going now. I do need to make my deposit to the Temple before this day is over." said Mr. Obed. I truly thank you again for your well-timed assistance. I owe you a great favor!"

As I quickly thought about this and the ending of our discussion, I suggested to Mr. Obed that maybe we could meet again for tea.

"Oh yes, that would be a great idea Gestas! Let me tell you where my business is located and come to see me anytime. I think your idea to meet again is a marvelous one."

Ah yes, what a wonderful way to start what would soon become a new business for me. If Flavius Obed only knew the things that I will be planning for us. If he only knew.

Talia
(Dew from God)

It is that time of year when the women gathered at the Temple to celebrate Purim – the Jewish holiday which commemorates the Jewish people being saved from Haman. Temple laws did not allow women to worship alongside the men but they had established a time that women of the Temple were to read the scroll of Esther at Purim.

Purim is fun though and we usually have quite the time gathering all the girls and ladies as we read through the entire story. It's our custom that whenever Haman's name is read out, we will boo, and hiss, and stamp our feet on the floor. We also have these things called "graggers" which are noisemakers which just add more to the mayhem as well as the fun.

The four main obligations at Purim are to 1) listen to the public reading of the Book of Esther in the synagogue twice. 2) Once in the evening and then again the following morning. 3) Send food gifts to friends and 4) Give charity to the poor. It was a busy time for the women of the Temple to worship and prepare food gifts for the friends and the needy. My mother relies on me to help her gather and cook and then deliver our gifts to those in need. It's exhausting and especially because of my father's position at our Temple.

I always found the story of Esther amazing and enjoy the reading of the scroll. It's a story of opportunity, of love, and of strategy, and ultimately the rescue of the Jewish community of people! Do you know the story? Let me tell you.

Esther was as cunning as she was beautiful. It was the time after the Jewish people were freed from their exile of the Babylonians. The king of Persia, King Ahasuerus, decided that he wanted a new queen and began his search over the land. He discovers Esther, falls in love with her, and makes her his new queen. Mordecai, Esther's cousin, instructs her to hide her Jewish origins in order to keep her safe because Haman, the Royal Vizier, who hates Jews. Soon after Esther's coronation, Mordecai learns of a plot to kill the king, tells Esther, and then Esther reveals the plan to the king, thereby saving his life. The king is then indebted to Mordecai and Esther for saving him from this assassination.

Haman, the king's highest advisor, convinces the King that on the 13th day of Adar to exterminate all of the Jews in the kingdom. When Mordecai and Esther learn of this decree, Esther hosts a banquet and invites Haman to attend. At some point during the banquet, the king learns of the decree and that Haman wanted Mordecai to be put to death, the king orders instead that Haman be put to death.

But the decree that all the Jews must be put to death on the 13th of Adar was still in effect! The problem however, the king explains, is that he cannot change such an order given under his name. So Esther convinces the king that the Jews should have the right to defend themselves. King Ahasuerus agrees and allows the Jews to defend themselves in all parts of his kingdom on the 13th of Adar and a day of rest on the 14th. The Jews indeed protect themselves and are victorious. It is then, on the 14th day of Adar, that the Jewish people celebrate their salvation by giving to those in need, exchanging foodstuffs, and feasting among friends. It was Esther who saved the Jewish people from extinction and an example of how women can overcome adversity.

As the scroll was being read, I could not stop thinking of the foodstuffs we have prepared! The sweet and delicious aromas were in the air all around the synagogue and it was embarrassing to the point, because it was making my stomach growl in anticipation of actually eating some of these delicacies!

Lamb and lentils cooked in clay pots over the open fire pits and locusts cooked in pots filled with salty water. Lentil stew seasoned with coriander. Goats milk cheeses of all types served with warm barley bread, onions and olives. It was all so good and I truly was ready and very hungry!

My mind was also on my friend Noam. He returned from his baptism with wonderful stories about this man Jesus. My father too, has seen this Jesus and shared some of his stories with me. I told Noam that he must include me on his next journey to wherever Jesus will be next. I have heard that Jesus has been traveling about and marvel at the stories of his healing powers I find unbelievable. How can a man heal people that are blind, paralyzed, possessed by demons? Noam also told me of the Spirit that descended down upon Jesus right after his baptism! What marvel follows this man!

Plus there was something different about Noam that I noticed since his return to our village. Certainly, he looked the same. Physically, there was nothing different about him, but there was a difference. Maybe it was the way he spoke? He seemed more confident. And there was this unmistakable sense of calm too. He seemed less harried and calmer. And it was attractive! I felt like I wanted, needed to spend more time with him as he told me about his experiences from that day he was baptized. His face lit up as he told me these stories and I found myself wanting to hear more and more. He also is pretty cute. Of course, that is my secret. I would *never* tell him how cute he is. No never!

Oh my, it is time to leave the synagogue! As the reading of Esther concludes, I am reminded of how she and Mordecai are such models of trust and hope for us. No matter how bad things get within our lives, they represent examples that God is committed to His people and will redeem our world. How wonderful our God is!

Leaving the hall I see him! There is Noam standing over there by the tree in the courtyard! He sees me now too. Oh my, he is smiling at me! He is holding something – maybe a gift for me? I feel like I would love to run over to him but I must not show him how happy I am to see him. And I know he's here to see me! This is really turning out to be a wonderful day indeed. What is he holding there? Oh that smile!

Petronius – The Centurion (Unsophisticated)

Capernaum. My home for the last 7 years. Located on the northern shore of the Sea of Galilee, it is a town bustling with merchants, fishermen and many farms surround our city of about 1,500 citizens. The inhabitants are mostly Jewish and they are a good people. Of course there always exceptions, but my centuries are well trained and have kept order amongst the people.

As a Centurion, I command a single "century" which is 80 men. We are part of a "legionary cohort" consisting of a total of six centuries. My century operates along the western side of Capernaum and we police the merchants and their markets and keep order in the town. I am responsible for training, discipline, and commanding my century. I love my job and actually have come to love the citizens of Capernaum and they too respect my men and me.

"Qen, bring to me my sandals! I must leave soon!"

Qen is my servant and has been so for the last 10 years. When we marched through Pelusium, Egypt, I took him into my service as my servant. He is a good man and I respect him and treat him as my brother, and not a slave.

"Qen, please hurry! Is there a problem?"

"I am coming Petronius, sir. Albeit, rather slowly these days. My illness seems to be making me sicker these past few weeks. I don't have the strength nor the energy anymore like I once had. I'm very sorry sir."

"Very well, Qen. It's just that I have an important meeting with the Temple leaders to discuss their complaint about a man they are calling Jesus. I have heard he is a rabbi from Nazareth and apparently, according to them, a troublemaker. They have told me that he came to the Temple courtyard and released many of their animals from their pens and upset the moneychanger's tables. Clearly, they are very upset about this incident and they have stated that I must meet with them to hear their complaints."

Qen replied "master, it would appear that the leaders at the Temple and their influence is being challenged by this Jesus fellow, don't you think? You have an unusual position with these Temple leaders as they hate the Romans, yet they respect you."

"Yes, Qen, I believe yours words are truthful. I believe it is better to try to accept their culture and beliefs than force Caesar's will upon them. Of course, my first duty is to Caesar and will always be, but I enjoy Capernaum being a restful community without conflict and disruption."

"It was wise and gracious master," Qen went on to say, "that you helped them build their Temple with your financial contributions. As you know, the Jews really do not like, nor accept, the gentiles into their fold. They only accept fellow Jews and you should be quite impressed that they have accepted you so graciously sir. Especially because you are a Roman Centurion!"

"Such is the truth Qen. But it was easy to see that they were influenced by my contributions not because of who I am. I was simply a means to their end. For me, I suppose it too was a means for me to gain their trust and mostly their cooperation."

As I laced up my sandals and finished dressing in my military attire, I glanced over at Qen who was now seated and appearing gaunt and exhausted from this simple task of assisting me in dressing.

"Qen, go now. Rest up and I will return after my meeting and after making my rounds with my men."

"Thank you sir. I am so grateful for you and I must say that you have become my slave and I your master. My illness has changed the ways things are supposed to be! Most slave owners would have me shackled and sent to debtor's prison by now! You have been so kind to me and I am so grateful!"

"Qen, you are like a brother to me. I simply cannot be unkind to you especially during this sickness that has come over you. You have been such a good and faithful servant to me these past twelve years. I worry now about your failing health so please, go rest while I'm away. Please rest."

Qen bowed his head, turned and began his walk back to his quarters. As he was shuffling along, he called back to me "thank you sir! You are such a good master!"

I turned and walked out the front door of my home. I decided that today, I would walk the streets to the Temple, gather my thoughts about exactly what the Temple leaders will say and want from me, and just "feel" the mood of the people. It is often said that a good leader walks amongst his people. This is how you learn of the things on their minds and get a reading of the pulse in the community.

It is different leading my soldiers as a centurion. As a centurion, they must listen and act with my every command. We are one unit and everyone must do as I say. There is nothing else for me to say after that; they must obey my every command even if they doubt it being the best order. They *must* obey me. That is the way.

I am brought out of my thoughts by the baker's display stand here on my path.

"Good morning centurion Petronius! May I interest you in some fresh bread? Or maybe a bowl of hot porridge this morning?" said the merchant.

The aroma emitted from his booth filled my nose and melted my stomach "no, not today my friend" I replied. I loved this walk. The street merchants were working on their crafts searching for customers for their works. There were glass workers, and potters and leather workers, and weavers alongside the "fullers". The fullers were the ones who cleaned and textured both old and new cloth. There is so much activity and the streets were alive with activity!

Most of these merchants were once peasants working the mines, and fields, but through their own labors moved into the city to sell their wares. Their particular craft skills had been taught to them and that was about their only skill they possessed. Most of them could not even read or write. Taxation weighed heavily upon the citizens, as funds were always needed for maintenance of the roads and public works, and of course, to feed our armies. The taxes under the current system, developed by Herod, which remain in effect, are threefold. First a tax for Rome, next, a tax to the local Governor, and then came the tithes and offerings to the Temple and the priests. Our Emperor Tiberius, has maintained peace amongst the people, however it was the local governors who had a difficult time keeping the peace amongst its citizens.

When Pilate was appointed Governor, several years ago, he was not a very popular person at all. It was Pontius Pilate that upset the Jews when he and his troops marched into Jerusalem at night and took over rule of the city. To further the drive into his unpopularity, Pilate then had an aqueduct built in Jerusalem which caused a conflict with the Jews because Pilate used Temple funds that had been set aside for sacrificial offerings to God. Of course, this caused uproar among the Jews and they revolted. In response to the revolt, Pilate disguised his troops as commoners and slaughtered the Jews in the Temple courts while they were protesting.

Judea seems to be always in turmoil. It is a rich land and one that is filled with history. As I approached the Temple, just recently completed, I cannot help but be amazed at its beauty and its stature. This magnificent building surrounded by wonderful courtyards is truly inspired by God almighty. Every time I see it, I am awestruck by the vision it took to create it.

Suddenly, I am jolted from my thoughts when I heard my name being called.

"Centurion, centurion, may I approach you sir? My name is Gestas. I would like to inquire about this scoundrel named Jesus." I find myself staring at this man wondering who he is. He continues to tell me what he's so aggravated about. "All by himself, he virtually destroyed these Temple courtyard grounds and many of us lost a lot of money from his deliberate actions! What do you plan to do about reprehending this, this Wildman?"

Gestas
(To complain)

"But you ask, 'How are we to return?' Will a man rob God? Yet you rob me? But you ask 'How do we rob you?'

"In tithes and offerings. You are under a curse – the whole nation of you – because you are robbing me. Bring the whole tithe into the storehouse, that there may be food in my house. Test me in this", says the Lord Almighty, "and see if I will not throw open the floodgates of heaven and pour out so much blessing that you will not have room enough for it." (Malachi 3:8-10)

"It is you O priests, who show contempt for my name. But you ask 'How have we shown contempt for your name?'

"You place defiled food on my altar. But you ask 'How have we defiled you?' By saying that the Lord's table is contemptible. When you bring blind animals for sacrifice, is that not wrong? When you sacrifice crippled or diseased animals is that not wrong? Try offering them to your governor! Would he accept you? Says the Lord Almighty." (Malachi 1: 6-8)

In some regard my fortunes, or should I say luck? Through my subsequent meetings with Mr. Obed, I have successfully negotiated an agreement with him for me to be one of the Moneychangers. It was he who was able to find me a very good spot for my table within the Temple courtyard. I have to admit, Mr. Obed knows a lot of the "right" people. He is a shrewd business man for sure.

He offered me an opportunity to act on his behalf as a moneychanger. He would cover all of the expenses here in the Temple courtyard and I would be able to keep 20% of the profits from the money changing. I know it's not a very good deal for me, but it's a start. I like taking the pilgrim's money. I like the profits I make. Someday, I will have enough money to secure my own table here at the Temple, but I am happy. For now that is.

Let me explain. Passover is the greatest of all of the Jewish festivals. Any Jew who lived within 15 miles of the Temple was obligated by Jewish Law to attend the annual festival. Of course, Jews from all parts of the land would also come thereby increasing the population of Jerusalem to over 2,000,000!

The males over the age of nineteen had to pay a Temple tax which was one half-shekel which is equivalent to about two days wages. This tax had to be paid in Jewish coins which were Galilaean shekels or in shekels of the Temple. Someone needed to make this money exchange and they are called the moneychangers. The moneychangers charge a fee to convert the Roman coins into those acceptable to the Temple. The bottom line for us moneychangers was a single transaction was equivalent to a days wages. It was a very respectable profit to be made for sure!

So here I am at my table in the courtyard and I am thinking, "who is this Jesus guy?" He came here yesterday. What a commotion He made! I would have demanded his arrest but He escaped before the soldiers got here. What a spectacle it was! He came through the Temple courtyard and was overturning all of the tables! He set free many of the doves and pushed the sheep out of their pens letting them free! From what I have heard, a lot of money was lost from his actions! What a commotion there was with yelling and shouting, almost screaming! This Jesus was yelling something about this should not be happening in his father's house? That this was not a place of business. But the Temple courtyard is a business!

Business is business, right? The Jewish priests want "perfect" offerings for the Temple sacrifice. Perfect? That is hard to produce right? I mean, HOW do you find a perfect dove? A perfect Sheep? According to their Jewish laws, the Jews must offer a *perfect* sacrifice to atone for their sins, that's how it works ok? But we are talking upwards of 200,00 sacrifices this festival week. Where can these vendors come up with that many "perfect" animals? So, the vendors compromise. They just simply bring what they have. Hardly a sin, right? Something is better than nothing right? I mean, let's be real about this whole thing, ok? Do they really think there is a God? Does God really exist in this miserable world? Everywhere you look there is strife. The beggars, the lame, the oppressive Romans, there is poverty, the Jewish are prejudiced against the gentiles, and so it goes. Is this Jewish God so righteous that He allows this to happen? Yet the business of purchasing sacrificial animals is booming as is mine of being a moneychanger. It's a profitable business and I am enjoying the prosperity that it brings to me.

But my day is lost now! The Temple has been cleared and there is no need for my services as a moneychanger today. Everyone is upset and has gone for the day now. I'm not sure what to do now with the rest of my day, but I do need to go pay Mr. Obed on the profits we made! This damn Jesus has hurt me. This was going to be a very good day working the crowds! Now they are all gone. Who is he? Some are saying that He is God! Can you imagine? God? Huh.

I do know a place though, where I can go later tonight. It's a place right near the Temple where they get drunk on wine and tell stories (that are likely untrue) and laugh and seek out the ladies. You know them, right? They are the whores. Everybody needs to make money right? But for me, it's a great place to pick pockets. After several cups of wine, these men lose their senses and are disoriented. Those are my targets! I am good at what I do! They are fools. Sinners come to atone yet they sin while they attempt to be forgiven. I really don't care. I am here to take their money. Period.

I just keep thinking of how this Jesus is so bad for business. What does all of this matter to him anyway? The Temple is a place of business; a big business. Just look around to see the numbers of tables with vendors, and animal pens surrounding the Temple within its courtyard! Then Jesus was telling the Jewish leaders, there at the Temple, some crazy notion that the Temple will be destroyed and that it would be rebuilt in 3 days?! I'm not exactly sure what *that* was all about.

(John: 2:13-22) *"When it was almost time for the Jewish Passover, Jesus went up to Jerusalem. In the Temple courts he found men selling cattle, sheep and doves, and others sitting at tables exchanging money. So he made a whip out of cords, and drove all from the Temple area, both sheep and cattle; he scattered the coins of the money-changers and over turned their tables. To those who sold doves he said, 'Get these out of here! How dare you turn my Father's house into a market!'*

His disciples remembered that it is written: 'Zeal for your house will consume me.'

Then the Jews demanded of him, 'What miraculous sign can you show us to prove your authority to do all this?' Jesus answered them, 'Destroy this Temple, and I will raise it again in three days.'

The Jews replied, ' it has taken forty-six years to build this Temple, and you are going to raise it in three days?'

But the Temple he had spoken of was his body. After he was raised from the dead, his disciples recalled what he had said. Then they believed the Scripture and the words that Jesus had spoken."

"Well, look here" I find myself saying, "here comes just the man I want to speak with –

"Centurion, centurion, may I approach you sir? My name is Gestas. I would like to inquire about this scoundrel named Jesus. All by himself, he virtually destroyed these Temple grounds and many of us lost a lot of money from his deliberate actions! What do you plan to do about reprehending this wildman?"

Jacob
(May God Protect)

"Ah my friend, it is so good to see you again! Thank you for giving me lodge this evening for it has been a long journey under a relentless sun!"

"Jacob, Jacob, please no mention of it! I am so happy to see you too! It has been too long" replied Nicodemus. "You must stay with me until you are rested. Come let us share some food together. I will summon the slaves to prepare us a meal."

"That would be wonderful, my friend!" You are such a scholar, and the Sanhedrin should learn a lot from your wisdom."

I followed Nicodemus into a smaller room just off the kitchen area of his home. As a Pharisee, Nicodemus was quite wealthy and could afford such a grand residence as this. It was beautiful and very comfortable. And after such a long day, it is wonderful not only to see my old friend again, but to be able to stay in his home is fantastic for me. What an honor.

"You know Jacob, I went to visit that nephew of yours! He has made quite the impression upon the Jewish leaders, and not in a good way either! He visited the Temple just last week and upset the tables in the Temple court and set free many of the sacrificial animals. I heard it was pandemonium and the Sanhedrin were not happy at all with him."

"Nicodemus! When was this?"

"No more than a week ago. He told the Jewish leaders that he would rebuild the Temple in just 3 days and they thought him a fool."

"Jesus is here?" I asked.

"Oh yes, he certainly is! Let me tell you of my meeting with him after the spectacle at the Temple. I learned of where he was staying and went there that evening. As you may suspect, his whereabouts is a closely held secret as he is not popular in every circle these days. Some want to even kill him for what they are calling his blasphemy." Yet, I believe he is more than what the people believe he is. I have studied his path and his words and his deeds throughout his travels, and I believe that he may be of what has been prophesied in the Torah."

"Jesus? My *nephew*? Son of Mary and Joseph? My goodness Nicodemus. I know that he is a special boy, well eh, a special man now, but what could he be from in prophesy? He is a very good student and has amazed other Rabbis of his teachings, but you think he is more than a Rabbi?"

"Well, Jacob, Let me tell you of my visit with him. I waited until the moon was up in the sky and traveled to the home where he was staying, and quietly knocked on the door. I was greeted by a couple of his companions and after a few questions of me, they let me in. And there he was, Jesus, relaxing by the fire. We exchanged greetings and discussed many of the things that were happening in Judea and how things seemed to be so unsettled.

We discussed how the Sanhedrin and the Pharisees and Sadducees were all too powerful, and sliding away from the ways of God, and more of what their own interpretations were of the Torah. They seemed more interested in creating wealth for themselves and their own synagogues than helping those in need. They have gotten lazy in accepting sacrifices that are faulty and not pure. They just want the money, the status and the power. Over the course of the time we spent together, he spoke of the Kingdom yet to come and the one here right now.

So I asked Jesus, *"Rabbi, we know that you are a teacher who has come from God, for no one could do these miraculous signs that you do unless God is with him. Jesus answered, 'I assure you, unless someone is born anew, it's not possible to see God's kingdom."* Then I asked Him, *"How is it possible for an adult to be born? It's impossible to enter the mother's womb for a second time and be born, isn't it?"*

"Jesus answered, 'I assure you, unless someone is born of water and the Spirit, it's not possible to enter God's kingdom. Whatever is born of the flesh is flesh, and whatever is born of the Spirit is Spirit. Don't be surprised that I said to you 'You must be born anew.' God's Spirit blows wherever it wishes. You hear its sound, but you don't know where it comes from or where it's going. It's the same everyone who is born of the Spirit."

So I asked Jesus How are these things possible*?*

"Jesus answered, 'You are a teacher of Israel and you don't know these things?

I assure you that we speak about what we know and testify about what we have seen, but you don't receive our testimony. If I told you about earthly things and you don't believe, how will you believe if I tell you about heavenly things?

No one has gone up to heaven except the one who came down from heaven, the Human One. Just as Moses lifted up the snake in the wilderness, so must the Human One be lifted up so that everyone who believes in him will have eternal life.

God so loved the world that he gave his only Son, so that everyone who believes in him won't perish but will have eternal life.

God didn't send his Son into the world to judge the world, but that the world might be saved through him.

Whoever believes in him isn't judged; whoever doesn't believe in him is already judged, because they don't believe in the name of God's only Son.

This is the basis for judgment: The light came into the world, and people loved darkness more than the light, for their actions are evil. All who do wicked things hate the light and don't come to the light for fear that their actions will be exposed to the light.

Whoever does the truth comes to the light so that it can be seen that their actions were done in God." (John 3:1-21)

"Jacob, I was amazed by what He told me; truly amazed! It is now that I believe that Jesus could actually be of the foretold; the Messiah."

I was listening to Nicodemus while he spoke, and also thinking of what I was hearing, and I truly had to think about the real meaning of his words. It was then I thought of the wind. The wind comes from somewhere and we don't really see how it blows, yet we can all *see* what it does. The leaves on the trees move from it, the dust whips up on the roads from it, the sails on the boats are filled and move them from it. I think that is like the spirit he speaks of. We don't understand *how* it works, but we can see the effects of a spirit-filled person upon others. The spirit has the power to actually make a bad person into a good person!

At that very moment and I began to see how all of this was coming together, I arose from my seat and immediately fell to my knees, and began to pray to God. "My Lord, you have blessed us indeed", I began. "You *have* sent your Son to save us! The scales have been on my eyes and I failed to see or understand that it was the time for the prophesy to be fulfilled. From that very first moment when my son Joseph told me that an angel had visited him when Mary was with child, and he knew it was not his own. This was *Your* Son, my Lord! All praises to you, my God! It is You who has sent Your Son to be with us; to save us; to see You in the living flesh!"

Nicodemus looked at me and came over and placed his hand on me while I continued to pray.

When I finished praying, we both took our seats near the fire. "My friend Jacob, I am sorry but I never asked you. Why have you come here?"

"I am here, trying to locate Jesus, to tell him the news."

"And what news is that Jacob?"

"Nicodemus my friend, I am trying to locate Jesus to tell him that his earthly father, my son Joseph, has died."

Talia
(Dew from God)

As I got closer to Noam, I could see his brilliant teeth sparkling in the sunlight and that infectious smile framed by his black and curly hair! Oh just the site of him makes me happy. But I must remain coy and uncaring to his eyes. I could never reveal the joy I feel in my heart that it brings to me to be in his company.

"Hi Noam! Why have you come here to the synagogue?"

"To see you, of course Talia! And. I have brought you a gift!"

He takes what he's holding and gently reaches towards my now cupped hands and then places it in my palms. I look down to see what it is. It was a cup made of chalk stone, a vessel, used for drinking. It was beautifully carved and so ornate. Not too ornate, but intricate enough that one could see it was very special.

"Oh Noam, it's beautiful! My goodness, where did you find it? It is so beautiful! Thank you, thank you!'

"Talia, you are very welcome my dear friend! I found it in a market in Capernaum and I felt, well, I just knew you'd like it. Well, I hoped, that is, that you'd like it."

"Like it? I *love* it! Whenever I use it I will always think of you Noam. It's such a wonderful and thoughtful gift. Thank you, thank you, thank you" and I gave him a gentle hug.

"Come, let us sit under the olive trees and I'd like to tell you of my adventures since my baptism." Noam said to me.

I felt like Noam seemed so much different to me since his return from his baptism. He seemed more confident, and stronger with his presence. He has a sense "joy" that just emanates from his body and he seems happier.

"Yes, Noam, please tell me! I have heard that this John the Baptist continues to travel about and baptizing many, many people. My father has also told me of his travels. What can you tell me about John?"

"It's actually a little hard for me to describe Talia. It was truly an amazing feeling and afterwards, many of those baptized were gathered in small groups. In some, we prayed. In others they discussed their feelings about what had just happened to them. But all of them, we all talked about love; true love for one another."

Noam shifted his weight and looked to the sky above. "It was kind of weird but we spoke to each other about love and loving one another. The kind of love of when you love someone dearly, you are willing to give it to them freely, and not even think about yourself. We felt like when you truly love, you are putting all of your trust and confidence into that love and into that person. And that's the way God loves us, and wants us to love and trust Him the same way. Does this make any sense to you Talia?"

"I think so. The Torah tells us to love one another, but you seem to describe it in a new way."

"Yeah that's it Talia, like a new way. And now, Jesus has found 12 men, what he calls disciples. They are with him and travel with him across our region. I have heard that these disciples are also going off helping John with the baptisms. It's really amazing! There are so many people flocking to be baptized that these 12 disciples are needed to cover much of Judea! Talia, there is newness in this movement and it's infectious."

(John 3:22-28) *"After this, Jesus and his disciples went out into the Judean countryside, where he spent some time with them, and baptized. Now John also was baptizing at Aenon near Salim, because there was plenty of water, and people were constantly coming to be baptized. An argument developed between some of John's disciples and a certain Jew over the matter of ceremonial washing. They came to John and said to him, 'Rabbi, that man who was with you on the other side of the Jordon – the one you testified about – well he is baptizing, and everyone is going to him.'"*

To this John replied, 'A man can receive only what is given him from heaven. You yourselves can testify that I said, 'I am not the Christ but am sent ahead of him'.

(John 3: 31-36) *"The one who comes from above is above all; the one who is from the earth belongs to the earth, and speaks as one from the earth. The one who comes from heaven is above all.*

He testifies to what he has seen and heard, but no one accepts his testimony. The man who has accepted it has certified that God is truthful.

For the one whom God has sent speaks the words of God, for God gives the Spirit without limit. The father loves the Son and has placed everything in his hands. Whoever believes in the Son has eternal life, but whoever rejects the Son will not see life, for God's wrath remains on him."

"Talia, in our lives, the truth for us is what God says is the truth. No Roman soldier, no Pharisee, and certainly no Sadducee! God is our truth without prejudice and it is He who loves us without condition. But is us, you and I, that need to commit to Him, be aware of Him in our life, and to choose Him first over anything."

"Noam, you have spoken so clearly and with such passion! I feel God is in you and you are His advocate. It is wonderful to hear you speak with such eloquence and devotion. It is so beautiful the way you speak!"

"Talia, thank you! I was maybe a little afraid to tell you of my feelings and my faith that I have found in God. I thought that maybe you would think I was being weird and not like the other guys who might be your friends. I just feel like I want to learn more about Jesus and the things that he is doing. It seems like the world is on fire with his teachings, and these miraculous things that he is doing throughout Judea are amazing. Have you heard of the crowds that follow him just to even touch his garments? He seems to be greater than a king! He is a healer too!"

"Shush Noam! You shouldn't say those things so loudly. Herod's spies are always around us. Herod is a paranoid and only craves power and gold. I hear that he is a very jealous ruler and we must be quite in our admiration of Jesus!"

"Shush back Talia. Now you are the one who is speaking too loud", as Noam was chuckling and smiling at Talia. "I think we will be great friends Talia, I just know we will."

Jacob
(May God Protect)

It wasn't that his trail was hard to follow, it was trying to make headway through the crowds that were following him! Simply the numbers of people trying to see Jesus, to touch him, to be healed by him, and to hear his words and teachings! I feel a sense of such desperation amongst the people that I have never felt before.

Likewise, I have never seen someone draw people to himself the way Jesus does. It truly is like he IS a king and the people flock around him just to be in his presence. I can attest to that in my walk today. I feel like a cow amongst a fantastic herd only able to shuffle along, shoulder to shoulder, without a means to increase my pace. It is hot and the road is offering nothing but dust suspended in the air that we are breathing and our tongues are parched.

My mind has been spinning since I left Nicodemus' home. My quest remains the same; I must re-unite with Jesus to tell him of his father and to simply be with my grandson for as much time that he can give me. And now, with all of this news of the things he is doing and saying, I am amazed how things have accelerated in his life.

As someone shuffles past me I ask "Excuse me sir, do you know the next town that we will pass?" I am so hot and very tired and almost near exhaustion; I must rest these weary old bones of mine.

"I believe it is called Zebulun, my brother. Will you continue to walk with us this evening? I have heard that Jesus is meeting, what he calls disciples, in a few days by the sea."

"I think not, for I must rest. I will continue afterwards. Thank you my friend."

Zebulun. I do pray that they will have a room available for me to stay in this evening. My feet are weary and my stomach empty. How did I get this old anyway?

I remember that time when we all went to Jerusalem, shortly after Jesus' birth, to have him circumcised. It was about a 5- or six-mile journey from Bethlehem to Jerusalem so we traveled together as a family. It is our tradition to dedicate our firstborn to the Lord who then will serve God throughout their lives. It was such a meaningful time for us and then we met this man at the Temple. Simeon. Yes that's right, Simeon.

(Luke 2:25-35) *"Now there was a man in Jerusalem called Simeon, who was righteous and devout. He was waiting for the consolation of Israel, and the Holy Spirit was upon him. It had been revealed to him by the Holy Spirit that he would not die before he had seen the Lord's Christ. Moved by the Spirit, he went into the Temple courts. When the parents brought in the child Jesus to do for him what the custom of the Law required, Simeon took him in his arms and praised God, saying:*

'Sovereign Lord, as you have promised, you know dismiss your servant in peace. For my eyes have seen your salvation which you have prepared in the sight of all people, a light for revelation to the Gentiles and for the glory to your people Israel'

The child's father and mother marveled at what was said about him. Then Simeon blessed them and said to Mary, his mother:

'This child is destined to cause the falling and rising of many in Israel, and to be a sign that will be spoken against, so that the thoughts of many hearts will be revealed. And a sword will pierce your own soul too.'"

"Hello good sir. Might you have a room for me at your Inn?"

"Oh yes sir" he said to me thankfully. I was so very grateful. And exhausted!

"It is a fine room and my only one left. These crowds certainly have helped my business and I've not seen so much demand for water, food and rooms in my entire life! Times are good for me. Praise God!"

My room was great. At this point, a donkey's stall that needed cleaning would have been great, so this room I rented for this evening was fantastic! A straw-filled sack, a window for the stars to shine through and upon me, and a door for a little solitude. The innkeeper served a wonderful porridge and my stomach was just as happy as I. Evening is fully upon us and before I lay upon the straw mattress, I kneeled and prayed to God, thanking him for my day's safe travel, a warm meal, and a roof over my head. Soon after, I easily drifted off to sleep.

My sleep was restful, up until this very moment at least and now, for some reason I am restless. I believe that it is still in the middle of the night and many hours before the sunrise. So many things are rushing through my brain right now and sleep is the farthest point away from my body. But I want to sleep! I am weary. I want to rest for I have another long day ahead of me. Following Jesus is exhausting! Yet I feel a sense of joy about it all. I cannot wait to see him again!

My thoughts change to what is happening now in Judea; well actually everywhere I can think of! Many times, when I have these sleepless moments, I go to the Lord in prayer. I hope he forgives me as I am lying down instead of being on my knees, but prayer is prayer, isn't it? Plus, often He rewards me with carrying me away to a nice deep slumber somewhere during my partitions. It's a good tradeoff He grants me.

For some reason I cannot tell, my mind is flooded with the Torah and the Book of Daniel. Has that ever happened to you? You are lead to a certain prayer, or to a favorite Psalm, or to a certain chapter in the Pentateuch? I believe that that is God's hand directing you to His words, His lesson, His thoughts. Tonight, He has lead me to Daniel.

Daniel is a great reminder for us that God wants us to be faithful, despite us being persecuted by evil people. He wants us to be patient and understand that it will be His timing when His reign will come upon us; and that God's Kingdom will come to humble the arrogant kingdoms of *this* world and finally we will have His healing justice which will reign forever!

Daniel. Yes, he was taken away from Jerusalem by the Babylonians. It was the Babylonians who attacked and plundered the city and then filled the Temple with their idols in a disgusting disregard for what is Holy to us. Then they took multitudes of the Israelites back to Babylonia to become slaves working in their mines and on their projects. It was Daniel, Shadrach, Mesach and Abednego, all Jewish leaders, who were fortunate because they were selected to work within the Babylonian Royal Palace. They were the exception and glad for it.

Although they were able to hold good positions within the Royal Palace, they were under constant pressure to give up their Jewish identities. But they held fast and true holding onto God's laws and not those of the Babylonians.

Over time, within the palace Daniel became known for being able to interpret people's dreams. It got to be well known within the palace that it was Daniel who could help you understand the things you dreamt about. One day the Babylonian king, who was troubled by his own dreams, learned of Daniel's talents and summoned Daniel to his court.

Daniel listened to what the king told him about his dreams and explained that the king's dreams were a warning that there will be many invading forces forthcoming who will attack his empire, filling their world with violence and upheaval. But Daniel also explained that one day it will be God's Kingdom that will come and rule the world.

Daniel had his own dreams too. In one of these dreams, he sees an arrogant king who exalts himself, even over God, and persecutes God's people! In the dream, God comes and destroys this king and exalts the Son of Man. And it is this new king whom now sits at the right hand of God and rules over all of the nations.

In another dream of Daniels, there is a Ram who represents the kingdoms of the Medes and Persians, and a goat who represents the ancient Greeks. This goat attacks Jerusalem, defiles the Temple, and makes claims of being even more powerful than God!

As Daniel ponders what this dream means, he wonders when something like this could happen and remembers the scroll of Jeremiah declares that the Babylonian exile will only last 70 years. It is then that an angel visits Daniel to inform him that Israel has yet again rebelled against the Laws of Moses and their oppression will continue seven times *longer* than Jeremiah envisioned.

Daniel has a similar dream again, but this time, this king whom has exalted himself above God comes to ruin. One day, God will confront the arrogant ruler, the one who glorifies his own power, and destroy him. It is this arrogant ruler who had defined for the people what is right and what is wrong, and did not acknowledge that God is the One true King! It is only God who can and will rescue the world and His people.

As I am lying there, sleepless and in awe of Daniel's message for all of us, I also wonder *where* God has gone? It's been over 400 years since we have heard from a prophet of God who will bring us news of His coming and bring us peace and salvation. Or is the Torah just a story that we hope is true? Do we have that kind of faith? Do I have that kind of faith?

Is that what Jesus is doing now? Giving us a message of hope that one day, God will push aside these arrogant rulers who believe that it is they who are the greatest, and they determine what is right and what is wrong? Have I become a doubter that God will come to save us from these rulers?

That is my last thought until I awaken to the crow of the rooster.

Petronius – The Centurion (Unsophisticated)

Centurion, centurion, may I approach you sir? My name is Gestas. I would like to inquire about this scoundrel named Jesus. All by himself, he virtually destroyed these Temple grounds and many of us lost a lot of money from his deliberate actions! What do you plan to do about reprehending this wildman?"

"Yes you may approach – Gestas did you say?"

"Yes it is sir, yes Gestas is my name. This Jesus, well he just went berserk at the Temple and scared everyone away! The day was totally lost because of his actions! We need to have him arrested for such a disruption!"

"As a matter of fact, I am looking into this matter you have described. I am on my way to meet with the Temple leaders and to hear more about this incident. So Gestas, did you actually meet this man named Jesus?"

"No, centurion, I did not. It happened so quickly. And then when he released the animals, and the doves ……why it was pure pandemonium! And with his shouting and the commotion that was going on, no one actually had a chance to speak with the scoundrel."

"I see Gestas." Well alright then, I must be on my way."

As I resumed my walk to meet the Temple leaders, my mind is full of the things I have heard about Jesus! These things that I have heard are quite difficult to comprehend. I wonder if they are true or simply exaggerations. Such is the human tendency – always make things larger than they actually are. Just here within the last few days I have heard this account from many who live here:

Luke 4:31-37: "Then he went down to Capernaum, a town in Galilee, and on the Sabbath began to teach the people. They were amazed at his teaching, because his message had authority.

In the synagogue there was a man possessed by a demon, an evil spirit. He cried out at the top of his voice, 'Ha! What do you want with us, Jesus of Nazareth? Have you come to destroy us? I know who you are – the Holy One of God!'

'Be quiet' Jesus said sternly. 'Come out of him!' Then the demon threw the man down before them all and came out without injuring him.

All the people were amazed and said to each other, 'What is this teaching? With authority and power he gives orders to evil spirits and they come out!' And the news about him spread throughout the surrounding area."

"Centurion Petronius, Centurion Petronius!"

As I looked back to from where I could hear my named being yelled, I recognized one of my house servants running very quickly towards me. He had a panicked look on his face and I could see that he was very upset. "What is it Malik? What are you doing here?"

"Sir, it is Qen! I am afraid he is almost dead! I went to his cot and I thought he may have been asleep, but when I approached him, he did not startle and his body was rigid – like he was no longer breathing or anything! Then I knelt by his side, and placed my hand over his mouth and yes, he was barely breathing! Plus he has a very high temperature; his body is racked with fever. You must come back to the house and help him!"

"Malik, I need you to return the our home and try to keep him cool with wet rags! I will get there as soon as possible but I have a meeting with the Temple leaders on another matter that I must attend. I gave my word to them that I would be there and now I am late. Please do as I say and I will be there as soon as I can. Go now, Malik, I need you to do this quickly! Go!"

I entered the Temple gates and then on to the meeting place, and I greeted the Temple leaders and elders according to custom. "Gentlemen" I said, "before we discuss what it is on your minds, I do have a favor to ask".

Luke 7:2-10 "There a centurion's servant, whom his master valued highly, was sick and about to die. The centurion heard of Jesus and sent some elders of the Jews to him, asking him to come and heal his servant.

When they came to Jesus, they pleaded earnestly with him, 'This man deserves to have you do this, because he loves our nation and has built our synagogue.' So Jesus went with them.

He was not far from the house when the centurion sent friends to say to him: 'Lord don't trouble yourself, for I do not deserve to have you come under my roof. That is why I did not come to you. But say the word, and my servant will be healed. For I myself am a man under authority, soldiers under me. I tell this one, 'Go' and he goes; and that one, 'Come' and he comes. I say to my servant, 'Do this', and he does it.

When Jesus heard this, he was amazed at him, and turning to the crowd following him, he said, 'I tell you, I have not found such great faith even in Israel.'

Then the men who had been sent returned to the house and found the servant well."

Noam
(Tenderness)

I have spent these last few weeks working on the docks, helping unload the nets of the fishermen. It is hard work but I do earn a slight wage for my labors. I am blessed as well because whomever I work for that day, sends me home with a few fish for me and my family for that evening's supper. I feel lucky and grateful to have such opportunities in my life!

The docks are also a great place to hear the many stories about Jesus! It's the merchants who arrive at the docks to purchase the daily catch, it is then we hear their stories about the miraculous things that Jesus has done and where he has traveled to and where he is heading to next. They speak of the huge numbers of people following him; so huge that most cannot actually even see him. These crowds form to actually resemble a human wave just in the hopes to have their sickness healed or whatever their ailment is. It sounds so amazing!

"Noam, Noam", I hear someone calling me. Oh now I see who it is. It's Talia's friend Miriam. She can be quite the busy-body and is always looking for the latest gossip. But she's a good friend of Talia's so I tolerate her. I wonder what can be so important today because she's running towards me. And she *never* runs! And she *never* has been seen in a fishing village for sure! This is very strange for her to be here!

"Hello Miriam! What brings you here on this fine day? And running too? My goodness you seem to be in such a hurry!"

"Noam, Noam I'm so glad that I found you! It is Talia! She is not well; not well at all!"

"What do you mean?" I ask. Miriam looks so concerned and so anxious to me. What does she mean 'she is not well"?

Miriam went on, "I was visiting Talia at her home and well, you know, we were just talking about girl-things and about some of the cute boys we like to talk about. Which, by the way, she really loves that vessel you gave her! She went on and on about what a unique and thoughtful gift it was. We were just enjoying some of the dates and oranges her mother had sliced and sat there talking about everything. But as we were talking and giggling, she went pale all of a sudden. Her eyes started blinking very fast, and I was like - what is happening here? Then she just sort of closed her eyes and rolled onto her side kind of like she had just passed out!

I screamed! I didn't know what to do! Then her father, Jairus, suddenly appeared and went to Talia's side. He tried to revive her and then laid her flat on a table. He yelled out to some of the others from the synagogue to come help him. Talia wasn't moving."

As Miriam was telling me all of this she started to cry. I put my arms around her to comfort her and I am thinking what has happened to my Talia? It sounded so sudden – one minute she is fine, and the next she has passed out; or even worse? What can I do? I knew the only thing that I could do; the only thing Miriam and I could do at this moment was to pray.

"Miriam, come kneel with me. Let me lead us in prayer for Talia. We must pray to God and ask for His healing hand to be placed upon her!"

"Then a man named Jairus, a ruler of the synagogue, came and fell at Jesus' feet, pleading with him to come to his house because his only daughter, a girl of about twelve, was dying." (Luke 8:41-42)

"Then one of the synagogue rulers, named Jairus, came there. Seeing Jesus, he fell at his feet and pleaded earnestly with him, 'My little daughter is dying. Please come and put your hands on her so that she will be healed and live. So Jesus went with him." (Mark 5:22-24)

"While Jesus was speaking, some men came from the house of Jairus, the synagogue ruler. 'Your daughter is dead', they said. 'Why bother the teacher anymore?' Ignoring what they said, Jesus told the synagogue ruler 'Don't be afraid; just believe.' (Mark 5:35-36)

"He did not let anyone follow him except Peter, James and John the brother of James. When they came to the home of the synagogue ruler, Jesus saw a commotion, with people crying and wailing loudly. He went in and said to them, 'Why all this commotion and wailing? The child is not dead but asleep.' But they laughed at him.

After he put them out, he took the child's father and mother and the disciples who were with him, and went in where the child was. He took her by the hand and said to her, 'Talitha koum!' (which means, 'Little girl, I say to you, get up!'). Immediately the girl stood up and walked around (she was 13 years old). At this they were completely astonished. He gave her strict orders no to let anyone know about this, and told them to give her something to eat." (Mark 5:37-43)

Talia
(Dew from God)

"Where am I? What happened to me? I was just sitting there enjoying the fruits and dates, and now I am sitting with Jesus?! Father, what has happened?"

My father, Jairus, is looking at me with absolute joy on his face; his smile shows me a simple look of wonderment and of awe! And then he casts his eyes upon Jesus, who is also smiling at me. I feel like I am in some kind of show or something; an object of great attention! Both Jesus and my father are looking at me and my mother is fixing us more food. And then Jesus smiles at me, and say "eat my child; you must be hungry."

Actually, I AM hungry! So we all begin to eat what mother has prepared for us. It tastes excellent and I feel thankful that I am eating; like somehow my body is craving for nourishment.

"Talia", my father begins to say, "we were so worried about you! You just seemed to pass-out for no reason, and we could not wake you! Everyone we called here to see if they could help us, were convinced that you were dead! Many wailed at the thought that you had left us and truly had died. I could not believe that such a thing could happen like this and I ran to seek the whereabouts of Jesus! And I found him! Not too far from here and begged him to come save you; to bring you back to us. Thank you again my Lord, for the blessing of saving my daughter!"

"Father, what do you mean that I was dead?"

"It is nothing my child" Jesus said. "You were simply asleep and now you are well."

As I looked at Jesus, he smiled with such reassurance and appeared to be so relaxed and comfortable. "Let me tell you a story," said Jesus.

"A man was going down from Jerusalem to Jericho, when he fell into the hands of robbers. They stripped him of his clothes, beat him and went away, leaving him half dead. A priest happened to be going down the same road, and when he saw the man, he passed by on the other side.

But, a Samaritan, as he traveled, came where the man was; and when he saw him, he took pity on him. He went to him and bandaged his wounds, pouring on oil and wine. Then he put the man on his own donkey, took him to an inn and took care of him.

The next day he took two silver coins and gave them to the innkeeper. 'Look after him,' he said, 'and when I return, I will reimburse you for any extra expense you may have.'

Which of these three do you think was a neighbor to the man who fell into the hands of robbers?" (Luke 10:30-36)

My father, Jairus, was the first to answer. "Jesus, what I see here is that we are ALL neighbors, correct? It should not matter what race, or color, or even religion someone is, a man in need is a man in need! This is the true core of love!"

I was amazed. I was amazed by this story because everyone knew that the Jewish people did not like the Samaritan people. It went back to the days when the Jewish people were exiled from our lands and the Jews from the northern kingdom intermarried with non-Jews. These were the Samaritans. And here was this Samaritan man, simply helping someone without prejudice! It was simply an act of love!

I said to Jesus – "The robbers were wrong because they knew they could overcome the man easily and commit an awful crime. To the innkeeper, it was simply business and an opportunity to make more money. However, the Samaritan took such action to help this man purely as an act of love!"

Jesus looked at my father, and then to me. He stood from the table where we were eating, and smiled. He placed his left hand over my father's hand and then his right hand over mine and said "Go and do likewise." (Luke 10: 37) And then he left our house.

Noam
(Tenderness)

Somewhere between the small town of Zebulun and Naphtali is Peter's house. I learned that Jesus liked to stay with Peter whenever he was in and around the Sea of Galilee. Jesus and Peter often traveled together; well I suppose they would, as I have heard that he is one of the disciples of Jesus.

I find it interesting that Jesus has picked this area to be around, conducting his teachings and his healings. This area around the northwest side of the Sea of Galilee is predominately filled with gentiles; the Jewish population is not that large here. My father believes that Jesus likes to be here away from the Sadducees and the Pharisees and their religious influences upon Jerusalem. I guess I think that this area is fertile ground, more accepting for Jesus to tell the people of the "kingdom" he keeps referring to.

Even though the crowds follow him like he is a king himself, my father has told me that not all people understand exactly what Jesus means or doubt the things he says could possibly be true! On the other hand, the things that he is able to do are miraculous! Making a lame person walk? A blind person can see again? Those who are possessed with some type of mental delusions are cured? He is amazing!

And Jesus *always* tells the people – "be faithful. Your faith has healed you. Because of your faith, you are healed." And he tells everyone "Go back home to your own people, and report to them how much the Lord has done for you and how He has had mercy on you." (Mark 5: 18) The word continues to spread among our people on these things that Jesus is accomplishing; I cannot wait for a chance to actually meet him!

My father told me today, that he will take me to the Mount within the next few days. This is where, it is rumored, that Jesus is gathering his disciples (this is what he calls them) to teach them more about this thing he calls the "gospel". Oh my goodness what an opportunity that would be! I can hardly imagine what it would be like to hear Jesus speak in person!

I am now beginning to understand something even more about Jesus, more deeply in my soul. I am getting a real sense that he is showing all of us a whole *new* way to worship God. We should be less ritualistic about *how* we atone for our sins. We should be more aware of others and their needs. And when Jesus heals these people and says to them "your sins are forgiven", I'm starting to understand that each person's life was greatly in need of getting "right" with God *first*. Those that have been healed by Jesus needed more than just a physical healing; they need a spiritual healing!

It was like what happened to that paralyzed man that was healed just last week in Capernaum. I'm beginning to see that this crippled man's greatest need was to be *forgiven* – not necessarily to have his legs enable him walk again! When Jesus said to him "your sins are forgiven" (Mark 2), Jesus knew this man needed to get his soul fixed *first*. To heal him spiritually first, get closer to God first, then we can start getting everything else moving is a positive direction.

It was also interesting that some of our synagogue leaders were very, very upset at what Jesus did there healing this man. They were accusing him of blasphemy against God because *only* God, God alone, can do such things. On the other hand, it was Jesus who was showing these religious leaders that He has the authority to forgive sin! Which leads me to my confusion – *who* exactly is Jesus then? He refers to God as His Father in heaven, so does this possibly mean that Jesus could be the Son of God? Is that why He is often calling Himself the *Son of Man?*

"A few days later, when Jesus again entered Capernaum, the people heard that he had come home. So many gathered that there was no room left, not even outside the door, and he preached the word to them. Some men came, bringing to him a paralytic, carried by four of them. Since they could not get him to Jesus because of the crowd, they mad an opening in the roof above Jesus and, after digging through it, lowered the mat the paralyzed man was lying on. When Jesus saw their faith, he said to the paralytic, '*Son, your sins are forgiven.*'

Now some teachers of the law were sitting there, thinking to themselves, 'Why does this fellow talk like that? He's blaspheming! Who can forgive sins but God alone?'

Immediately Jesus knew is his spirit that this was what they were thinking in their hearts, and he said to them, '*Why are you thinking these things? Which is easier: to say to the paralytic, 'your sins are forgiven', or to say 'Get up, take your mat and walk'? But that you may know that the Son of Man has authority on earth to forgive sins....*" He said to the paralytic, '*I tell you, get up, take your mat and go home*'. He got up, took his mat and walked out in full view of them all. This amazed everyone and they praised God, saying, "We have never seen anything like this!" (Mark 2:1-12)

I can't wait to see Jesus!

Machaerus
Hell on Earth

Machaerus. That is what it is called. The real-people call it "hell on earth". It is someplace that no one wants to go to. It is a place to fear and everyone knows that very few ever leave there. And it is where John the Baptist has been for these last two years as a prisoner.

Machaerus sits atop a very high hill just to the east of the Dead Sea located in a small village named Mukawir. It was originally built as a fortress because of its strategic location to see approaching military threats and it offered a very difficult terrain for any attackers. However, it was destroyed by the armies of Pompey in 57BC. That is until Herod the Great had it rebuilt and used it for his army to safeguard his territories around the Dead Sea. He then passed it onto his son, Herod Antipas, its current owner.

In the middle of this vast complex sits the royal palace where Herod Antipas lives with his second wife Princess Herodias and her daughter Princess Salome.

It was Herod Antipas who was responsible for putting John the Baptist in this awful place, imprisoning him for the last two years. And what crime did John the Baptist commit? Was it unlawful to baptize people in the name of the Lord? Was it unlawful to assemble such large crowds of followers throughout Judea? Was it unlawful for people to praise this John the Baptist man and give them new hope and a new spirit? No, none of this was unlawful.

It was Herod Antipas who was afraid of John the Baptist! The crowds of followers were simply amazing and Herod feared the influence that John was having over his people; Herod Antipas' people! These were his constituents and it was his power that would reign over them! I'm sure he was thinking that if these followers of John ever assembled together, they could revolt against his reign and destroy his small empire. And there was another reason why Herod Antipas had to take John the Baptist off the street – John the Baptist told these crowds that Herod illegally divorced his first wife Phasaelis, according to the laws, and then married his brother Herod Philip's wife! Herod surely thought that no one should dare speak out against their king like this! This had to come to an end!

"As John's disciples were leaving, Jesus began to speak to the crowd about John: 'What did you go out into the desert to see? A reed swayed by the wind? If not, what did you go out to see? A man dressed in fine clothes? No, those who wear fine clothes are kings' palaces. Then what did you go out to see? A prophet? Yes, I tell you, and more than a prophet. This is the one about whom it is written:

I will send my messenger ahead of you,
Who will prepare your way before you.

I tell you the truth: Among those born of women there has not risen anyone greater than John the Baptist, yet he who is least in the kingdom of heaven is greater than he. From the days of John the Baptist until now, the kingdom of heaven has been forcefully advancing, and forceful men lay hold of it. For all the prophets and the Law prophesied until John. And if you are willing to accept it, he is the Elijah who was to come. He who has ears, let him hear.

To what can I compare this generation? They are like children sitting in the marketplaces and calling out to others:

> *We played the flute for you, and you did not dance;*
> *we sang a dirge, and you did not mourn.*

For John came neither eating nor drinking, and they say, *He has a demon.* The Son of Man came eating and drinking, and they say, *Here is a glutton and a drunkard, a friend of tax collectors and sinners.* But wisdom is proved right by her actions." (Matthew 11:7-18)

Both John the Baptist and Jesus were upsetting the status quo of the thinking of the people – *all* of the people. Jews, gentiles, the religious leaders and the political leaders! The requirement for following the teachings takes courage, faith, endurance, and likely changes in the way we live because there are always those, including ourselves, who doubt and are afraid to lose their own power.

And Herod Antipas was being threatened. "But when John rebuked Herod the tetrarch because of Herodias, his brother's wife, and all the other evil things he had done, Herod added this to them all: He locked John up in prison." (Luke 3:19)

They met regularly, Herod and John. Of course, what choice did John have? He was a captive under Herod's control. Herod actually liked John and truly enjoyed his teachings. Herod knew that John was smart and well spoken about things most people really didn't understand. And in Herod's own deviousness, he was using John for his own purposes.

"Tell me again John, about this man Jesus" asked Herod. "I hear claims that he is a prophet, and then I hear that he will bring forces from above to destroy me and the entire Roman army. I have heard he has these special 'powers' to heal people from their infirmities and has even brought the dead back to life?"

And so it would go between them. "Tell me of this 'new' kingdom Jesus will bring into Judea." Or "What happens when a Jewish person dies; where do they go? Is there really just one God? Why would you believe that? Why is everyone following Jesus and not you?" The questions would go on and on as did their meetings.

Herod would like these meetings or 'sessions' to be quiet and almost secretive there at Machaerus. Herod did not want others to know of their meetings especially his wife. Herod also knew that he could never let John go free. There were just too many people that loved John and followed him and he was too afraid that John would begin a resurrection against him. He was trouble and he could never let John leave his prison.

Over time, Herod eventually did allow John some visitors; some of his disciples. These disciples would tell John about what was happening throughout Judea and mostly about this prophet named Jesus. Of course, John remembered baptizing Jesus and how God spoke to them at the moment Jesus was baptized. John was very interested in these things that Jesus was doing.

John was expecting his cousin Jesus to be the Messiah who would come to judge and reward the faithful and punish the wicked. To seize power and establish a new kingdom here on earth and destroy all enemies including Rome! Both he and Jesus were miracle babies and they had their roles to fulfill according to God's plan.

And so it was that one day John's disciples were at the prison visiting him when John asked them to seek out Jesus. You see, John was expecting something more of this Messiah. A real king, a powerful conqueror, a ruler who would save the Jews as well as the entire world! So he directed his disciples to find and ask Jesus "Are you the one – or should we expect someone else?"

"Now Herod had arrested John and bound him and put him in prison because of Herodias, his brother Philip's wife, for John had been saying to him: 'It is not lawful for you to have her.'

Herod wanted to kill John, but he was afraid of the people, because they considered him a prophet.

On Herod's birthday the daughter of Herodias danced for them and pleased Herod so much that he promised with an oath to give her whatever she asked. Prompted by her mother, she said, 'Give me here on a platter the head of John the Baptist.'

The king was distressed, but because of his oaths, and his dinner guests, he ordered that her request be granted and had John beheaded in the prison. His head was brought in on a platter and given to the girl, who carried it to her mother. John's disciples came and took his body and buried it. Then they went and told Jesus. (Matthew 14:1-12)

John's earthly mission had been completed. He was set aside from the very beginning when the angel of the Lord told Zechariah and Elizabeth that they would have a son, who would not be in any form of power or a person of a political nature. John's Godly mission was to speak and deliver His message of the truth, for the people to repent of their sins, and to be born again in their new lives after being baptized.

And it was there, in a monstrous fortress, surrounded by evil, and filled with sinners, that John's mission came to an abrupt conclusion. As we are beginning to understand, God does not guarantee an easy, safe life for those who serve Him, and we are beginning to understand the importance of *truth*, which is more important than life itself.

Jesus did respond to John before he was beheaded and told John that He was doing the work of God in healing the sick, curing those who were faithful, that "yes" Jesus was the Messiah, that He was teaching the people how to love one another and to be faithful to God as He is to us. We all need to *trust* Jesus, follow Him, believe in Him, even when things are not going the way we expected them to go!

And John died knowing the truth – the Messiah has finally come!

Jacob
(May God Protect)

I am close to him now! I have traveled his path and heard of the things that he has done, and said, and of his teachings. I have heard that he has assembled a team of friends that assist him in every way. Well, he calls them disciples but they appear to behave like a team learning and getting stronger in their cohesiveness.

I continue to be amazed at the crowds that surround him and, actually, slow him down. His followers resemble something akin to the largest herd of sheep ever assembled in history! I cannot even describe what this is like but I know I am getting closer to where he walks. I can feel his energy and his spirit and know he is close by! It has been too long since we last spoke, and now it is difficult for me to think of how it will be when I tell him of his father's passing.

Gestas
(To complain)

I have settled my debts to Obed and have left the Temple grounds. I am not complaining. Well, maybe I am. It was just too boring a lifestyle for me. I just could not satisfy the *beast* that is inside me. The beast requires me to steal, to hurt, to beat, and yes, even to murder. I was thirsty and so is the beast.

I am not a religious man; I don't believe there is an actual God. If there is, then someone needs to prove to me that there really is a God. What I do know is there isn't one in my life and I can say there never was one in my life. Ah yes, my life! I am the living proof that there is NO God!

I was born into this world by people that did not deserve to be called parents. For as long as I can remember, (or is it more like since I began remembering?) I struggled to survive. Those "parents" hated me. I clearly was just another mouth to feed, another body to clothe, and something to take care of. This was accentuated whenever they drank that cheap bitter liquid they called "wine". Then it got worse. And the older I got, the harder the beatings became to endure.

We were nomads really. Constantly moving from one village to the next taking, stealing, begging, whatever was necessary to survive. I had no friends, nor did I want any. I saw things that people did to people that was not human like behavior. And I always heard people saying that God will provide, and that we would be saved by him. I never saw anyone being saved by this God they spoke of.

One night, I snuck away from our "camp". I couldn't stand the beatings anymore and by now, I pretty much knew how to beg, swindle, cheat, lie and steal with the best of them. I left those people, who were once again in a drunken stupor that evening and I lnow they wouldn't even miss me until the next morning. I was 12.

It's funny. When you don't have parents that actually care about you and don't teach you about life, about right and wrong, about duties and responsibilities, and about accountability? You are lost. Well, unless you depend upon yourself, like I did. It's called survival! I learned what is necessary to survive in this world! I already knew it was a tough world, but I really hadn't seen it all. Not back then, but I know now! And what about this person who learned on his own how to survive? I actually came to enjoy it! It's fun for me to bring hurt and suffering upon the weak and feeble. It's exciting to instill fear into the innocents, take their wares and their money, and beat them into submission, maybe even taking their lives!

I laugh when they cry out 'God have mercy on me'! I ain't seen no god that has stopped me yet. Funny though, as I say that, I do remember a time in Egypt, when I attacked that caravan. They were just a young family and part of a small group heading south. I had my great hiding area in that valley and I sprung to attack them. I remember it was a young couple with an infant child. I heard him yell "Mary stay in the cart with the baby!" There was so much screaming going on and I was ready to attack, and then I don't remember what happened. The next time I remember anything I was laying on the sandy trail; it was nighttime and I was laying there with a large lump on my head. I never knew what hit me. Never found out either. It's still a mystery to me.

"Why are you telling me all of this Gestas?" Jairus asks me. "You have come to this synagogue, under your own free will, to tell me that you do not believe in God? You have come to a place of worship to spill out your hatred, confess your sins, and tell me of some of your crimes? What is it really that you want?"

"I want to know where God is Jairus? Is he hiding in *this* synagogue? Is he hiding behind that curtain over there? Has he saved anyone from death? **Where is he Jairus?**"

"Over 400 years ago, there was a prophet named Malachi, an oracle who delivered a message to the people. You see, an oracle is a message from God Himself, and He spoke to us through Malachi" explained Jairus. "Our people, the Jews and likely the rest of the world, became hardened about God's love for us. They assumed that the world was run by the politicians, by the government, and their individual success was measured by their own economic wealth. It was a great time of spiritual apathy, my friend. The people lost their awe of God and became self-focused on their own problems and forgot about loving God!

Malachi tells us in Chapter 1, verse 2 "I have loved you, says the Lord." but you see Gestas, the people stopped loving Him! Their hearts no longer had Him in them; they had been blinded and influenced by earthly things and they were not *faithful* to God's law. The people treasured their own words and ideas, and not God's words.

Gestas, we were born to follow Him! He wants *your* love. And it should start with forgiveness. Your testimony about your life? Forgive your parents. Remove the hate from your heart; give up your idols that consume your energy and time; soften your heart as it has become hardened by your own pride; careless living without being God-centered leads to disastrous consequences!"

"So I ask you Jairus, who is this man they call Jesus?"

Jairus began "I am not quite certain Gestas. I have heard great and miraculous things about him. I hear of the things he says and of his teachings. In my heart, I am beginning to believe that he is more than a prophet as some claim he is. He speaks about a "new" kingdom but I don't believe it's the kind of kingdom the people want right now. The people want, our people here, want a new leader and their own country. This is not the kingdom Jesus will be bringing. Based upon what I have heard and seen, I think He could actually be the Messiah, the Chosen One."

"Well, I don't see it that way at all Jairus! He's just another religious despot delivering fancy tricks to the distraught and giving hope where there is none!

Thank you for your time Jairus. I must go now. I believe that I am missing some of the best hours of the day for what it is I do."

So I left him at the synagogue. All that talk about God is exactly what it was – talk.

Acaph
(To Gather; To Harvest)

For the next 2-3 years, Jesus spends his time in the area of Capernaum and resides with Peter whenever he is close by. His public ministry takes Jesus to districts known as Zebulin and Naphtali which are located north and west of the Sea of Galilee.

Why these particular areas? These areas are mostly populated by gentiles and were far removed from the religious leaders in Jerusalem as well as their religious influence. Jesus would often call these religious leaders and their followers "poor in spirit". The poor in spirit were spiritually proud and self-sufficient rather than those who were seeking God and His plan for their lives.

As for the people? For the first time, or maybe the first time in a long, long time they felt hope. Hope that there actually was something for them to live for. That their daily toils had a meaning that traveled far beyond today. They found hope that someone actually heard their prayers and could help them. They felt a closeness to this God of the Jews and were encouraged that He wasn't just for them only. He was available to anyone who called upon Him!

But the greatest feeling felt was the one of JOY. Pure and unadulterated joy! There was joy in the simple act of giving to one another, even if it was as simple as speaking encouraging words, a heartfelt hug, an approving smile, giving a gift in a time of need. This selfishness brought joy somehow and it was being passed along via the words and actions of Jesus and His disciples.

It was Jesus who proclaimed *"I must preach the good news of the kingdom of God to the other towns also, because that is why I was sent."* And teach he did! He traveled and delivered the good news to the synagogues throughout Judea throughout the lands of the Jews. His messages were for all who would listen. Those who gathered, sometimes in the thousands, were amazed by his teachings and the things he did healing and casting out evil spirits.

Jesus taught about loving enemies with the same respect and rights we expect for ourselves. He instructed us not to be judgmental and not to criticize others and adopt a forgiving spirit. He reminded us that what's in our hearts and soul drive our actions and our attitudes. Our beliefs must be solid and built upon a firm foundation or we will easily be lead astray.

The message was clear and included all. Yes, even women. Under Jewish law, women were not supposed to learn from rabbis, yet Jesus included them in service and in fellowship. He was a messenger for all of the people regardless of status or health, in poverty or wealth, as a soldier or a commoner. His message was for all.

So Jesus appointed his 12 disciples. And then he assembled 36 teams of two to extend his reach to the people. As Jesus said *"The harvest is plentiful, but the workers are few. Ask the Lord of the harvest, therefore, to send out workers into his harvest field. Go! I am sending you out like lambs among the wolves."* (Luke 10:1-4) As followers of Jesus, we are asked to bring the good news, in his name, to the people of the world, and to pray for them. Introduce people to prayer and God will do the rest.

When the 72 returned, they were filled with astonishment over their accomplishments. That spiritual truth was for everyone, and God *is* for everyone regardless of their social status and we all need to trust in His grace for us.

However, as Jesus walked the land and delivered his message to the people, not all accepted his message. This included every type of person, of all stature, Jew and gentile alike. Many were afraid of the power they witnessed that Jesus had over the demons and his message to repent of the sinful their behavior. Many asked him to leave them alone and many wanted him dead. So too in the major city of Jerusalem the problem of Jesus was brewing among the religious leaders.

In Jerusalem, there were pretty much three main groups of religious leadership. The Essenes, the Pharisees, and the Sadducees.

The Essenes were communal in their personal lifestyles and discouraged ownership of personal property and money. They devoted themselves to the strict interpretation of the Laws of Moses and lived to assist others in need. There were many Essenes who congregated in many cities throughout Judea but not as large as the Pharisees nor the Sadducees.

The Pharisees strove to interpret the Torah literally and would often create new laws to explain what God really meant by the Laws of Moses. The result of their actions ended up promoting their own self-interests and aided them with corruption.

The Sadducees were the aristocrats. They liked the status quo and sought power and influence within the political arena. They only believed in the Torah and held that any other religious writings were blasphemous as well and assured that any new found doctrine would be rejected.

What Jesus is bringing to the world is certainly in conflict with the Sadducees and the Pharisees. Jesus is introducing a new way to be with God and opening up more participation in the new kingdom and away from the Jewish legalistic traditions. He has come to restore God's reign. He invites everyone to join His kingdom, regardless of their social status, and to spread the good news to all. As this message travels throughout Judea, it is clear the things that Jesus is promoting and teaching has become a very large threat to those religious leaders.

During these days, Jesus gathers the curious and his followers, and tells them how to live in God's Kingdom. The religious leaders are adamant that there is only one who can do the things that Jesus is doing and that is God. And this man named Jesus? He's *not* God. The religious elite fear the power that Jesus is amassing among the people through his works and teachings will end their reign and power among the people. The decision has been made and these religious leaders have begun their scheme. Jesus needs to be eliminated!

Noam
(Tenderness)

"Yes father! I did hear you – I AM packing!"

My goodness he can badger me! It's just that I don't want to forget a single thing for this trip. Our family is headed to Jerusalem to the Passover as are thousands of other people. It is such an important time for us as we celebrate the end of our slavery and escaping from Egypt hundreds of years ago.

Our trek to Jerusalem is about 80 miles so it will take us 4-5 days to get there from here. It's a long journey, and yet an exciting one, where we often meet new friends and reunite with old ones. And Jerusalem is alive! There are so many people converging into the city, with vendors and merchants, and magicians, and clergy, and so much food…….it numbs my mind in such a pleasurable way. I can't wait!

Plus, I'm pretty sure we will meet up with Talia's family too! Our friendship has grown in these last two years, I can only hope that she too feels the same way I feel towards her. She has grown into such a beautiful woman. I think others can see our friendship may be more than just friends – I know her father looks at me differently now. Like a watchful Sheppard making sure his sheep are safe. He's a good father.

As I turn, looking for my favorite tunic, I see my father standing in the doorway to my room. "Son, before we leave, I must sit down with you to discuss our journey."

"Of course, father. Is this the right time?"

"Well, yes of course Noam. I suppose it is. Please. Please, sit my son." We both sit on the edges of my bed and my father begins to speak.

"You are old enough now to fully understand the importance and significance of the Passover."

"Yes, yes of course I do father!"

"Yes, yes, I suppose you do" my father says. "I am a bit worried about the things I hear that are happening in Jerusalem and the mood of the people. There is energy in the air and it isn't all good. The people are tired of Roman rule and want change. They believe that the time is now for a new ruler and a new king for our lands. There is talk among so many that this prophet Jesus is that man who will bring the change people are calling for."

"Yes, father. I too have heard of these things. I know that there is much talk that Jesus will be there with us in Jerusalem and there are so many people waiting for his arrival."

"Son, this is what I really want to say to you – we must be careful! I have heard that the Romans, and that Governor Pilate are bringing in extra troops to quell any potential riots that may arise. These Roman troops do not have the patience for us and surely, they will react swiftly to any perceived threat. We *must* not give them any reason to raise a sword against us!"

"Of course not father! I would never give them a reason to lift a sword against me and our family!"

"This is what I fear Noam; that somehow we will be ensconced inside of a crowd and someone hurls a rock at one of the soldiers, or does something against them, and then the soldiers will attack the crowd seeking the perpetrator. And the next thing you know, we are caught in the scrum and someone in our family is injured or jailed! Simply by being caught in the wrong place at the wrong time!"

I could tell my father was getting very upset as his voice was rising yet almost in an excited whisper. The spit was flying out of his mouth with every other word and his face was getting redder.

"Father", I said, "please calm down! It will be alright. You and I will stay close and protect Mom and my sister. Do not worry. We will be vigilant and stay away from such trouble-makers. I promise you. We must have faith father! Faith in God. That He will look over us and guide us with whatever our problems are. God gave Moses the power to overpower Pharaoh, He delivered us from slavery and we were freed. And He gave us the wonderful opportunity to remember how He saved us – the Passover. We will be fine my father. Now let us go and load the cart for our journey!"

Pontius Pilate
(Skilled with a Javelin)

As I look ahead and turn to see what is behind me, it takes my breath away! My soldiers, armed and at the ready, march in rhythm with a cadence sounding thunderous to the crowds that line the street. The calvary upon their chariots and riding their massive steeds are impressive and so intimidating to everyone showing the people the power of the Roman Empire. It literally sends chills down my spine.

This year I have brought 1,000 legionnaires to reinforce our garrison at Fortress Antonia situated right across from the Temple. I expect no trouble once these fanatical Jews see the force that I bring into Jerusalem. There will be NO trouble, for that, I am positive!

Our procession on this Sunday seems to be even more attended than in previous years. Our westward journey has thus far been uneventful and we are arriving right on schedule. Petronius has done well leading his troops. As I look around to see the Golden Eagle mounted on the poles my men are carrying, and the beating of the drums, the sound of the march, all reminds me of the power I possess. The beat of the drums is now echoing off the buildings lining the streets and it sounds like thunder; manmade thunder that is! The thunder of the Roman Empire for all to enjoy!

"Isn't this exciting Pilate?" Claudia asks me. She looks stunning today in her white robe, her hair pulled back (in the way I like it) and adorned with her gold bracelets and belt.

Yes, my dear, it truly is. Look at all of these people cheering us and our arrival. It is there chance to see the power of the Roman army and of our empire! I must admit, I too feel the power we possess. No one can stand in our way! Listen to them cheer Claudia, listen!

"Pontius darling."

"Yes, my love, what is it?"

"Do you think that we might have a chance to meet that prophet? The one named Jesus?"

Petronius – The Centurion (Unsophisticated)

"Qen, I have received new orders! I have been ordered to report to Jerusalem to bring my soldiers and assist with keeping order during the Jewish Passover. They say that the crowds will well surpass previous years attendance."

Qen turns toward me with concern written on his face. "There is too much talk these days my lord. There is so much unrest among the people of this land and rumors of insurrection abound. Why do they hate the Romans so much?"

"Qen, they are a very religious people and have dreams about ruling their own people inside their own country. But they have no leaders and they have no armies to change anything. They claim to be waiting for their God to deliver a new king, one that will conquer any and all invaders in their lands. I understand their dream on this but it is very far from reality. I am from Rome and it is Rome that rules the world!

Qen, please assemble my things for this trip. I will likely be gone for about a month so please include the things I will need for this stay."

"Of course my lord."

I went and sat down at my desk to write out further orders for my men, and to sign off on any outstanding affairs that needed my attention. I couldn't help but to think about this man Pilate, to whom I will be reporting to. The things that I have heard about him reveal that his character is suspect for sure.

I know that he was appointed Governor and had a record of provoking the Jews and the Samaritans to the point of rioting. He was constantly initiating new laws to diminish Jewish privileges and flaunted Rome's rule over them. Naturally, the Jews despised him. I cannot help but feel that I will be entering Jerusalem under very strenuous circumstances! Will we be entering into a fight, a riot, a rebellion? I know not but I must be prepared for most any circumstance. I am a centurion after all – hail Caesar!

Jacob
(May God Protect)

I find myself quite mesmerized as I am listening to Jesus here in the synagogue. His teachings are so deep in meaning and there is so much to absorb into your mind, it is quite challenging!

"Move over Jacob."

Whispering, I say "Ah, it is you, Nathaniel!"

"Yes, yes of course, it is good to see you too my friend. I was hoping that I would find you here. It has been too long since we have been with each other! Way to long!"

Nathaniel leans further into me as we are seated here in the synagogue in Decapolis, also known as the Ten Cities. It is known that Jesus likes to preach to the Gentiles here because it is they who are in the majority in this region. Jesus is able to attract many, many disciples from this area and the Gentiles are attracted to him by his teachings, his kindness and of course, his healing powers.

"I have heard that so many of these Gentiles love these teachings from Jesus and are spreading his words throughout the Decapolis! They seem to be so ready for this Good News, Jacob. I must admit, it is quite infectious!"

"Nathaniel, shush. Listen as Jesus is telling another parable."

"Then the King will say to those on his right, 'Come, you who are blessed by my Father; take your inheritance, the kingdom prepared for you since the creation of the world. For as I was hungry and you gave me something to eat, I was thirsty and you gave me something to drink, I was a stranger and you invited me in, I needed clothes and you clothed me, I was sick and you looked after me, I was in prison and you came to visit me.'

Then the righteous will answer him, 'Lord, when did we see you hungry and feed you, or thirsty and give you something to drink? When did we see you a stranger and invite you in, or needing clothes and clothe you? When did we see you sick or in prison and go visit you?'

The King will reply, 'I tell you the truth, whatever you did for one of the least of these brothers of mine, you did for me.' (Matthew 25:34-40)

"You hear that, Jacob? Jesus is explaining that each of us does not need to be rich, or have certain abilities to help one another! We don't need to wait for the government or religious leaders to assist people that are in need or in crisis. Everyone, each person, each one of us, has the power to help each other. It is what is in our hearts and our souls that guide us to help each other. It is just as Isaiah has said:

"Is it not to share your food with the hungry and to provide the poor wanderer with shelter – when you see the naked, to clothe him, and not to turn away from your own flesh and blood?

Then your light will break forth like the dawn, and your healing will quickly appear; then your righteousness will go before you, and the glory of the Lord will be your rear guard.

Then you will cry for help, and he will say: Here I am." (Isaiah 58:7-9)

"Yes, Nathaniel you are correct. Jesus is softening the hearts of the people with these teachings. We truly must love one another, just as we love ourselves. He is able to open up our hearts to go beyond thinking just of ourselves and by doing these things for others? Our selfless acts glorify God! The people of Decapolis are embracing this and the Word is spreading. Better than that, the actions of the people is the true message. They are putting these teachings into their actions! It is so beautiful, isn't it?"

" Shhh Nathaniel, listen now, Jesus is talking about what will happen in the future. What it will be like to follow these teachings. Listen Nathaniel."

"You must be on your guard. You will be handed over to the local councils and flogged in the synagogues. On account of me you will stand before governors and kings as witness to them. And the gospel must first be preached to all nations.

Whenever you are arrested and brought to trial, do not worry beforehand about what to say. Just say whatever is given you at the time, for it is not you speaking, but the Holy Spirit.

Brother will betray brother to death, and a father his child. Children will rebel against their parents and have them put to death. All men will hate you because of me, but he who stands firm to the end will be saved." (Mark 13:9-13)

At that moment, Jesus stands and returns to the bench where the synagogue elders were seated. Jesus is finished for the day and the synagogue leader then leads us in prayer.

The crowds were so thick within the synagogue and those outside waiting for a chance to see Jesus, I was unable to catch up to him myself. My goodness, I just marvel at the crowds; it is difficult just to simply navigate back to my hostel. As I lay down and prepare for sleep, I think about all of the gifts that God has blessed me with this day. Such a beautiful day that I am so thankful for! God is great!

It was good to see Nathaniel again. After prayers we went to a local place to share some figs and naan bread. I find it so interesting that, at first, Nathaniel was skeptical of Jesus. His friend Philip had told Nathaniel that he had found this man Jesus of Nazareth, whom he believes is what Moses wrote about in the Law regarding the *Chosen One*.

To which Nathaniel said to Philip, "Nazareth! Can anything good come from there?" (John 1:46)

Then when Jesus saw Nathaniel coming toward him, Jesus told him *"I saw you while you were still under the fig tree before Philip called you."* And then told him that he was *"an Israelite in whom there is no deceit."* which astonished Nathaniel because Jesus *knew* his thoughts and his heart.

Ever since that moment, Nathaniel has believed that Jesus is the Christ. And now, as a chosen disciple of Jesus, Nathaniel always tells me of the stories of their travels together. I find myself mesmerized by the stories of the things Jesus has done.

I left Nathaniel and started my walk back to my hostel. The streets were still blazing with activities and the merchants were still selling their wares. Yes, there's nothing like Jerusalem during Passover. The atmosphere is just filled with activity, excitement, and, oh yes, the aromas of cooking soups and meats which is just overwhelming to my senses!

I think of my life and it seems so ordinary in comparison to many of my friends and acquaintances that I have met. I am just a simple man, leading a simple life. I wonder if I have done the right things and if God will grant me entry into His Kingdom?

I feel guilty because I am not always a faithful follower of Him. I find myself questioning or doubting sometimes about if there really is a God. It is so hard sometimes when you see the evil in this world and question "why" God allows these things to happen.

I see even the religious leaders use their power and influence to raise themselves above the people they are supposed to be helping and saving. They use their power to enrich their own lives. It is difficult at times to maintain one's faith. Forgive me my Lord, in my times of weakness.

Well, that was quick! I suppose my mind was so filled with my thoughts that my walk back to the hostel went very quickly for sure. I swing open the door and I am immediately greeted by the manager. "Hello Jacob! And how was your day?"

"Magnificent! It truly was a wonderful day. And, I got to hear Jesus preach at the synagogue! How good is that?"

After a short exchange with the manager, I climb the steps to my room, and wash the dust from my face. I am tired; very tired. But it is a *good* tired and I am ready to sleep.

I feel my eyes begin to flutter as sleep is quickly approaching. Yes indeed it was a very good day. My evening prayers are filled with color tonight. My heart is warmed and my spirit is lifted simply being in the presence of Jesus and to hear the Word and to see His works *together*. Sometimes I forget to be in awe of such a powerful and loving God, and Jesus reminds us of God's authority over our lives. We need to stay close to Him and understand His love for us! Praise be the Word of God. Amen. These are my last thoughts as I doze off.

Gestas
(To complain)

After my discussion with Jairus, I went back to who I was; a God-less thief who is looking out for myself, and only myself. I actually find it easy to prey upon these Temple-mongers and their insistence that there actually is a God who will help them.

God never helped them as I stole their money and jewelry. Or when I beat them, sometimes so seriously I left them unconscious. In many ways they are the weak ones. They succumb to worshipping something they have never seen. And they succumb to my brutality which is very real and very painful on top of that.

"So what are you in here for?" asks this man named Barabbas.

"I was caught by the Roman guards. They claimed that I was a robber, a thief they said, with multiple charges and multiple witnesses against me. It is not true, however. And what about you? What's your deal to get into this lovely place?"

"Some would call me a trouble-maker, some call me an insurrectionist. Truly as I speak to you, we need to take our lands back and rid ourselves of these Romans! All the way back to the time of Moses, God told us that these lands would belong to us. The Romans keep us from our God-given rights. So I fight them."

I look at him with a quizzical look on my face. "How do you fight? You are just one person. Are you crazy?"

"I organize. I organize men who have a similar passion to take our lands back. Then we scheme and gather. Then we attack small bands of the soldiers, cutting their throats, and steal their weapons for our next attack."

"Interesting. Interesting that you actually believe that you can conquer and expel the Romans from our midst with these small terroristic actions? So what did Pilate charge you with? Being a crazy lunatic?"

Barabbas scowled at me and stared at me for quite awhile. I wasn't sure if he was going to attack me in our prison cell, or decide to end our little conversation.

Finally, he began to speak again. "I am charged with sedition, insurrection, and treason which together carry a death sentence. I do not know when but I am to be crucified. Not a death I would have chosen for myself! I would have much rather died fighting than be pitched up in the air for all to witness. The men who fought beside me and along with me knew our efforts were valiant. They saw me slay many men over the course of the last two years, and my name is famous among the city. I am Barabbas!"

"Well Barabbas, you are now in jail, along with me in this cold, damp, disgusting cell, and are sentenced to die in an awful way. Being that we both convicted as murderers, we face the cross and likely together. I'm quite certain you know about being crucified, but do you know how you die from being crucified?"

"It sounds like you are going to tell me Gestas."

"I have heard that it was Alexander the Great who brought it back from the eastern Mediterranean countries and the Persians introduced it to the Romans. It is a brutal way to die lasting up to six hours until your body finally gives out and you either die of a heart attack or suffocation. The weight of your body pulls down on your arms, which will likely dislocate your shoulders, which then makes it extremely difficult to breathe. The 7" nails that are used to hold you up on the cross will sever the median nerve causing great pain and likely render paralysis in your hands.

Your feet will be nailed to the upright part, almost like a step, and your knees will be bent at a 45-degree angle giving your legs virtually no support for the body. Once your legs can no longer support your weight, the weight is then transferred to your arms. You getting the picture Barabbas?"

"I'm not quite sure exactly why you find all of this necessary to explain to me! I understand that I will be executed and that is all I care to know. I believe that God will bring me relief in some manner. I pray that He will forgive my sins as I know I broke His law when I killed those soldiers, and I seek His mercy."

"Ah yes, another 'God will save me' type. What fools you are! The last mention of God by a "prophet" has been over 400 years ago! He hasn't come down from the heavens and rescued anyone has He? He hasn't established any of His Kingdoms anywhere around here, has He? I haven't seen any angels flying in for a rescue of His people, have you? This God you speak of simply is an idol that these religious leaders use to abscond your money."

"I trust and believe Gestas that you are mistaken. God is what's in your soul and directs you down the right path. It is *us* that makes the wrong decisions, it is *us* that choose the wrong path, and then it is *us* that claim there is no God. We are all sinners with no exception, but it is God who loves us and wants us to love one another and to be aware of sin and stay away from it. Yes Gestas, we need God in our lives, and He does exist. Because if He doesn't then there is no reason for us to be alive."

"No more talking you two!" yells the guard from his post within this dungeon we now live in.

I lower my voice just above a whisper so I don't attract any more attention from the guard. "I guess I just don't get this whole God-thing. I'm tired of hearing about it! Then all I keep hearing about is this Jesus from Nazareth. Maybe he'll be the one who will rescue me. Ha. Sure he will."

Pontius Pilate
(Skilled with a Javelin)

I hate the Jews.

My father was a knight, a member of the equestrian order from Rome, and I was raised in a comfortable life style. I attended a small but demanding school with high expectations of their students. My favorite was mathematics, but I was well versed in reading and writing. And then came my time serving in the Roman army where I learned a fair amount about the Jewish people. They seemed to be everywhere in Rome and owned so many shops, and markets, it was stifling.

The Jews were the consummate businessmen and because of their success with trade and business, most were quite wealthy. Most Romans respected their life styles as they dedicated themselves to their God, and were well known for taking care of those in need. They enjoyed the respect given by Julius Caesar as he allowed them the right to worship their God instead of Rome's. It was almost like they were even in higher status than being Roman! This I resented very much.

I received my post as Governor of Judea, Samaria and Galilee in the year 26AD. It is about 1,400 miles from Rome and takes about 3 weeks to get to it. It is not a fun trip to make which maybe influenced my attitude towards the Jews. I am the fifth Roman to serve here in Caesarea in this capacity. My predecessor, Valerius Gratus also hated the Jews and the Jews hated him as well. He ruled with an iron fist and was known for crucifying any and all terrorists (mostly Jews) in the region. It was his preferred method for dolling out death punishments. Which made it an interesting transition when I took over; they immediately hated me and the feeling was mutual.

The areas that I govern, the people are extremely anti-Roman. They themselves have separate religious groups who, at times, are pitted against each other as to the severity of their views and interpretations of the Law of Moses. My job is to keep order, make sure taxes are collected, and improve and expand commerce in this region. My boss, the Emperor Tiberius, has ordered me not to stir-the-pot as they say and let the populous rule their own for the most part. Not an easy thing for me. I like order. Actually I demand it.

For the most part I have followed Tiberius's request to let them be as long as they are not breaking any of our Roman laws. So I allow the Sanhedrin to manage the civil duties of government and much of the law enforcement. It has worked for the most part. The Sanhedrin meet daily in Jerusalem at the Hall of Hewn Stones just on the north side of the Temple complex. It works for me.

Passover is right around the corner now so I will be heading to Jerusalem. I really don't go there often – it's such a big city and there are so many people – but I always go for the Passover week. So many people and there is always tension amongst the religious leaders and the Iscarii. Plus, there is no sea to view. Since I have become governor, I spend most of my time at my palace here in Caesarea Maritima overlooking the Mediterranean Sea. Beautiful blue waters splashing along a rocky coastline. So beautiful. Unlike Jerusalem where it's dust everywhere. I need security to be tight this year in Jerusalem and it is my job to oversee the security to make certain there is no trouble. This year, I have ordered more troops to make certain there is no trouble.

There is room at the Antonia Fortress for these extra centurions and it is located right across from the Temple. It provides an excellent point for observing what is happening on the streets below. Me? I will be staying at Herod's Citadel which is where I usually stay when I'm in Jerusalem. It's comfortable and my wife enjoys staying there.

I know the crowds that will appear for the Passover will overwhelm the city as usual. Thousands will come and the activities in and around the Temple are unbelievable. And the animals. The animals are everywhere, being sold to the pilgrims at exorbitant prices just so they can make sacrifices to atone for their sins. What nonsense is this? Clearly, this is big business for the Jews and a huge money-maker for the Temple.

I am suddenly aware of my day dreaming when my wife appears.

"Darling, how long do you believe that we will be staying in Jerusalem?"

My wife, Claudia Procla. Her love for me keeps me sane. She is smart, witty, and a good consultant for me regarding important affairs under my direction. Someone that I can trust and have a fair debate with. She is a good wife for me.

"Claudia, I do not expect any trouble during the Passover so hopefully, this trip will be no longer than a few weeks. However, I must be sure things are calm even after the hordes leave the city. The zealots seem to always be ready to incite a riot and even murder when large crowds assemble."

"Pontius, come now. Do not get yourself upset over these things. We cannot control the things that haven't even happened or may not ever happen. These thoughts just get you excited in put you in a foul mood! Please, my love, just calm yourself."

"Of course Claudia darling, you are right. Come sit with me for a few moments. Tell me your thoughts – what have you heard about this Nazarene named Jesus? What are the people in your circle saying about him?"

"Ah, Pontius. That is indeed a difficult question to answer. So many things are being said about this man. The things that I have heard are quite astonishing and the people's reactions are so diverse. Everyone wants to know *who* he is. Some hope that he is the long awaited Savior, the Messiah of the Jews and of the world, and the religious leaders here *fear* that he will take away their positions of authority as well as their power. Some fear that he will change their lives and bring judgment to their sinful lifestyles."

"Yes dear, I too have heard similar things. Do you think I should fear him Claudia? Will he organize the Jews and incite a call for change and spark a revolution against we Romans?"

"I don't really know the answer to that Pontius. I do feel though, that the message that he delivers throughout his travels has been one of love and caring for each other. His message seems to always be the same. Love God. Love one another as you love yourself. Take care of those in need. Be faithful that God has a plan for you in this life. These are good messages. I do not think they are words that will incite a revolution to overthrow our government, do you?"

"Forgive me sir for the interruption!" my personal guard says. As I look up, see my guard, it appears that he is quite excited and anxious. He knows that I hate to be interrupted and likely is nervous for the repercussion that it will bring.

"Yes, what is it?"

"Sir. Our spies have reported, what they have learned from multiple sources……."

"Out with it already soldier! Tell me quickly son!"

"Jesus has left the area of Mount Tabor and is on his way to Jerusalem."

"This is news? Of course he will be coming to Jerusalem! He's a Jew and it's close to the time of the Passover! This is what you have interrupted me over! There better be some *news* in this interruption soldier!

"Sir, yes sir, there is!" Our spies inside of Jerusalem are telling us there will be a great gathering, a significant sized gathering awaiting his entry into the city! The crowds could be so large that we may not be able to contain them if there is an uprising by the people, sir."

"Then I suggest that you prepare accordingly and bring in even more troops. That is all soldier! Do your job! You are excused."

As I watched him leave, and I look towards Claudia, I see the expression on her face. It probably matches my own. Something like – "hold-on, here we go into something that we know not what to expect, but it's not going to be good."

Micah
(Chapter 7:1-7)

"What misery is mine! I am like the one who gathers summer fruit at the gleaning of the vineyard; there is no cluster of grapes to eat, none of the early figs that I crave.

The godly have been swept from the land; not one upright man remains.

All men lie in wait to shed blood; each hunts his brother with a net.

Both hands are skilled in doing evil; the ruler demands gifts, the judge accepts bribes, the powerful dictate what they desire – they all conspire together.

The best of them is like a brier, the most upright worse than a thorn hedge.

The day of your watchmen has come, the day God visits you.

Now is the time of their confusion. Do not trust a neighbor, put no confidence in a friend. Even with her who lies in your embrace be careful of your words. For a son dishonors his father, a daughter rises up against her mother, a daughter-in-law against her mother-in-law – a man's enemies are the members of his own household.

But as for me, I watch in hope for the Lord, I wait for God my Savior; my God will hear me."

Petronius – The Centurion (Unsophisticated)

Another restless nights sleep for me. Our journey to the city of Jerusalem certainly was uneventful, thankfully. The roads were so crowded that it was difficult to keep our pace and remain on schedule. Of course, the people that cluttered the roads moved to the side of the road as we marched through them. Our cavalry men and the chariots made certain the path was clear as we marched.

The Antonia Fortress welcomed us in typical Roman form and it is good to see some of my old friends again. My quarters here at the fortress are small but comfortable. However, I cannot seem to find comfort in my sleep. I keep thinking about what the climate here in Jerusalem is like. I say "climate" not of the weather but of the "mood" of the people here. It feels like there is a storm coming. I can feel it. It's in the air. Like lightening and thunder. You know not where it will strike and you can feel the rumble of the thunder off in the distance.

Everyone expects the prophet Jesus is coming for their Passover festival. The people are excited about his coming. To be healed by him, to hear him speak about this new "kingdom" he speaks of, and his disregard of the Pharisees. He is challenging these Jewish leaders and questioning their teachings and interpretations of their God's laws. Plenty of tension in the air for sure. There is a sense of a storm brewing amongst these religious leaders between them and Jesus.

I have learned that the Pharisees love their rules, the commandments that must be followed, and the rituals that must administered.

And then there are the Sadducees who were wealthy and involved themselves in the local politics, working in close association with the Roman aristocrats and those in positions of influence.

Then, here comes Jesus who is definitely "stirring the pot" as they say. His message and teachings are less ritualistic and come more from a position of loving one another and discovering that the true blessings are the blessings that come from inside of you, the blessings of your own heart. Put these things into action and love one another as you love yourself.

There is also a storm brewing inside of me as well! I feel something within my own heart that is making me restless. I am being drawn into the things that I have heard about the teachings of Jesus. I am being drawn into this concept of one God, and that God is love.

Talia
(Dew from God)

I am amazed at the traffic as we travel the hard-packed gravel heading towards Jerusalem! There are very few breaks between the carts, and the pilgrims who shuffle under the banks of clouds. Regardless, there is excitement in the air. Passover has that effect on all of us. Of course it is a time of atonement and repentance, but it is also a time of reunion! In many instances friends and families are being reunited since the last gathering; since the last Passover.

My mother and I are riding in the cart – just to rest our feet for a few more miles. It is now the third day of our journey and this too has been a long day. But Jerusalem is not that far away now. The colt that pulls our loaded cart has done well but we mustn't over burden him with the weight of us riding in it along with the other items loaded in it.

My father has been in deep discussion with the man just ahead of us on the trail. As they have been walking, they talk and laugh on occasion, but I can tell they have been having a deep discussion, none of which I can hear from where I sit in this cart.

"Mother, do you have any idea what father has been discussing with that man up ahead of us?"

"Talia, why do you always have to know *everything?* If your father wants us to know, he will let us know."

"Mom. You must ask questions, constantly! Or you'll end up no smarter than this colt pulling us in this cart! I'm getting off this cart and finding out what is being discussed between those two!"

"Talia, wait!"

I climb off the cart (of course it's going so slow that there is no risk of falling or tumbling off) and I approach my father and this man.

"Father, who is this new friend you have made here?"

"Oh, yes Talia. Yes, yes, this is Jacob and he is from Gerasene, which is across the lake from Galilee. We were just speaking of a few things."

Then Jacob looks at my father, then to me, and then back to my father and says "It was nice to meet you Jairus and I enjoyed our conversation very much." and then he scampers ahead to meet up with his family just ahead of us.

"Father, why do men refuse to recognize women? It is very rude. I am a real person just like him and you!"

"Talia, you ask so many questions! Like I have explained to you before, our culture believes that women should be silent and just do as they are told. In our family, that is not always the case. I respect your mother, and now I respect many of the things you do and believe in too. The world is changing but slowly in this regard. You must respect this culture and be mindful when strangers are around."

"Oh my goodness father, what a world we live in! I should have been born a man!"

"You may be right Talia" as my father laughs. "You may be right. But you were not, thankfully. You are a becoming such a beautiful, wonderful woman and surely God is working inside of you weaving such a wonderful tapestry! It brings me such joy and happiness!"

"Thank you father! Now tell me, what were you and Jacob so intensely discussing? You must tell me!"

"Oh well, we spoke of many things but he told me a few stories about Jesus that I had not heard. Jesus sounds so interesting and the things he has done are simply amazing. Miraculous actually!"

"Yes, yes, please tell me father! Like what has he done?"

"Well, as I told you Jacob is from the region of Gerasene. Jesus had been on a fishing boat there at the Sea of Galilee and came to the shore. As he left the boat he was met with a demon-possessed man, naked, and living in one of the caves there on the shore. This man was shackled in chains and began to scream at Jesus not to torture him!

This man's name was Legion and the demon in him begged Jesus to send them into a nearby herd of pigs rather than being sent down into the abyss. Jesus agreed and the demons left Legion and went into the pigs! Then the pigs ran down the hillside and into the Lake and drowned!"

"This is a crazy story father! Who has ever heard or seen of such a thing? So, then what happened?"

"Well, the townspeople heard that the man named Legion had been cured, and that his demons went into the pigs and the pigs ran off the cliffs and drowned themselves. Seeing this, the people were afraid."

"Well surely they should have been!"

"Talia, and guess what they asked of Jesus?"

"Did they thank him for saving Legion?"

"No! They told Jesus to leave! They were afraid."

"Afraid? Afraid of what father?"

"Change. They were comfortable in their lives as tenders of pigs and secure in the revenue the pigs brought to them. You see? They valued the lives of the pigs more than a man's life. They were faced with the question of what is more important? Isn't a human life more important than money or the life of an animal? The people didn't want to give up their lifestyle and comforts they had even to save a man in need!"

"Oh my gosh, that is unbelievable! It is sad to hear this about the townspeople, but how is that possible the evil spirits entered into the pigs?!"

"Jacob also told me another story he had been told about another demon-possession. This time it was a boy. His father saw Jesus coming and cried out to him for help. The boy was this man's only son and he suffered from convulsions so bad that even sometimes he foamed at the mouth from these awful spells!

Jesus told the boy's father, as well as the crowd that now surrounded them, *'O unbelieving and perverse generation, how long shall I stay with you and put up with you? Bring your son here.'* (Luke 9:41)

And Jesus rebuked the evil spirit and the boy was saved and returned to his father."

"This is truly amazing father! Do you believe all of this is true? This Jesus must be......."

"The Son-of-God is what he calls himself Talia."

I am looking at my father with amazement. What does Jesus mean when he says Son-of-God? I can hardly understand, no I can hardly comprehend what that means! Does that mean God has come to our world in the form of a human-being?

My father is looking at me too trying to understand the look on my face, trying to figure out what I am thinking of all of this. I think we both truly do not know *what* to think!

"Jacob, the man I just met, told me something else that Jesus had said. Jacob believes now that Jesus is the Christ and that he is God. These teachings, and parables that Jesus speaks in, and all of these healings are demonstrating God's love for us! He told me that Jesus said –

"All things have been committed to me by my Father. No one knows who the Son is except the Father, and no one knows who the Father is except the Son and those to whom the Son chooses to reveal him." (Luke 10:22)

I am looking at my father. I'm not sure what to think about all of this. As a believer of my Jewish faith, we believe that God will deliver to us a Messiah. And now we are on our way to the memorial Passover celebration and I am beginning to wonder what if? What if this Jesus, the Son of God he calls himself, is truly our King? I scarce can take it in.

Noam
(Tenderness)

"Then the Lord said to Moses, *'Go down, because your people, whom you brought up out of Egypt, have become corrupt. They have been quick to turn away from what I commanded them and have made themselves an idol cast in the shape of a calf. They have bowed down to it and sacrificed to it and have said 'These are your gods, O Israel, who brought you up out of Egypt.'*

"I have seen these people," the Lord said to Moses, *"and they are a stiff-necked people."* (Exodus 32:7-9)

The journey was long, as expected, but the crowds were the largest I've ever seen. Father had his challenges navigating through the throngs of people but we made it! And our reservations were honored and we have settled into our accommodations. Father explained to me that quite often these Jerusalem inn-keepers will want to re-negotiate the prices previously arranged for. Especially this year as crowded as things are. But our inn-keeper maintained the agreement negotiated last year and my father is happy.

I can feel the tension that surrounds the city. The people here seem anxious and uncertain. The Temple is very busy and the money-changers seem to overwhelmed with the pilgrims. It is hard for me to imagine a sense of piety with the "business of the Temple". It seems more like a business than a place of worship and the priests are more interested in adding to the coffers of the Temple treasury than performing religious duties!

When I was reading my Torah this evening, and reading from Exodus, I was in awe because it seems like we too have strayed from what God wants for us. Other things in our lives have become *more* important than recognizing and worshipping our Creator. We create our own idols, things that we put before our relationship with God. We seek to have power, and influence, and be prideful in who we are rather than recognizing it is God who has made us in His own image and to BE like Him. It fills me with sadness when I think of how little we have changed in all of these centuries. Thankfully, God is patient and still loves us in spite of our sinful ways. What an awesome God!

Some of the things that I am hearing is that Jesus may be more than a prophet. The things that he says and does are unbelievable to me. Well not just me, many if not most are in awe of what he has been doing.

And now that we are here in Jerusalem, there is a different *feel* about Jesus. Many close to the Temple seem afraid of him and claim that he is committing blasphemy against God. They are saying that he is a sorcerer even.

So many things that we have been told about Jesus and his teachings, and his abilities to cure people from their ailments, simply often just by believing in him, through faith alone is amazing!

But how? How can a *man* actually be God? God in the form of living flesh? If he is God, why has He come now? What is his purpose for coming down from heaven? What will our future be like with God living amongst us? Is God here to oust the Romans from His lands?

"Noam! Noam, please come down from your room! You have a visitor."

Wow, I was so deep in thought I was startled when my father cried out! I want to think all of this through but I must go see who could possibly be here visiting me! How exciting to have a visitor in Jerusalem!

Talia
(Dew from God)

"Talia! Oh my goodness, what a surprise to see you! Oh, and yes you too as well Mr. Gilead, yes, yes, of course!"

I think it is so funny to see how nervous Noam gets whenever he is around my father! Oh my, I think Noam is *actually* blushing!

"Noam, it is so good to see you as well! When we learned where you and your family were staying here in Jerusalem, I told my mother and father we just *had* to visit!"

"Mr. Gilead, let me introduce you to my father, Samuel."

"Nice to finally meet you Samuel. Noam has told me much about you and your family. Please call me Jairus."

"Certainly Jairus. Please do come in and make yourself comfortable. The journey has been long for all of us; please have a seat."

As I steal a glance at Noam I can't help but notice how he has grown. It seems as if he gets taller and broader and even *more* handsome than the last time I saw him. His face was filled with such a joyous look to see me that I too almost blushed from my excitement.

"So Jairus, I am told that you have heard Jesus preach." asked Noam's father. "Do you find his messages confusing?"

"Hah, that is actually quite funny Samuel that you should say that. I must admit, at times it can be quite confusing to fully understand what Jesus means when he speaks certain lessons. His style for delivering a message is often called 'speaking in parables'. Frankly, it is so fraught with metaphors and wisdom, one really has to think about exactly what he said and its true meaning. It is interesting too that by him speaking in parables he is fulfilling prophesy for it is written "I will open my mouth in parables, I will utter things hidden since the creation of the world." (Matthew 13:35)

Samuel listened closely and then asked Jairus "Jairus, can you recall some of these parables in which you speak of?"

"Oh for sure Samuel. One of my favorites is known as the Parable of the Four Soils. I love this parable because it summarizes the components of faith and belief. Jesus tells us about a farmer who is spreading seed, very similar to what Jesus appears to be doing now. He is spreading the Good News about a new kingdom and for some people this is falling upon deaf ears while others are learning and growing from it."

I am listening to my father telling Samuel about these Jesus parables yet all I can think of is Noam, who is sitting right beside me. I want just to talk to him and hear some of his stories again and to have him make me laugh. So I poke Noam with my elbow and whisper to him "Do you think we could escape this talk and go outside for a few minutes Noam?"

Noam whispers to me "Let me ask my father."

"Excuse me father, would it be ok if Talia and I stepped out to the garden area for a few moments? We'd be just outside the door here."

"Well if it's ok with Jairus, then it is fine with me."

My father looks at Noam and I, then looks at Samuel, and finally says that he's ok with it too.

Noam and I go out the door and sit together on a bench looking out over the garden. Gardens are not typical in Jerusalem as space within the city is at a premium, but this rental house has a lovely one. Contrasted against the desert browns and tans, the greenery just explodes with majestic colors. It is quite stunning.

"Talia" I hear Noam saying to me. "Talia, I have something on my heart that I must tell you."

I look at Noam and he is looking at me so intently. My heart starts to flutter because I truly do not know what to think he might be so serious about.

"Talia, I might embarrass myself, but I have gotten to a point where I really don't care. I want to tell you what is truly on my heart – and I am afraid that I may be making a fool of myself by revealing it to you."

"My goodness Noam. What is it? You're actually making *me* nervous now. Is it that you don't like me or don't want to see me anymore? I'm sorry for coming over here tonight and pushing myself into your family gathering! But I just wanted to see you and hear more of your stories – just to have you talk to me."

"No Talia, that's not it at all! You didn't push yourself into me and my family! Actually, I am thrilled you did and delighted to see you here! I must tell you that I am so happy to see your pretty face and beautiful smile again. It's been too long since I saw you last! And that is what I have to say to you…..I have feelings for you! From the very first time we spoke to each other, and laughed, and just spent quiet moments together, I *knew* I wanted to spend more and more time with you! I think that I *love* you!"

Oh my gosh! What a moment. Noam is telling me what is on his heart. I feel my heart racing and I am so excited because that's exactly the way I feel too! My face is flush I'm quite certain because it feels hot. My blood is rushing through my body and I feel so happy. I feel so happy because I feel the same way. I feel what I think love should feel like!

I say ever so softly, "Noam, I feel the same way towards you too! I'm not sure what love is supposed to feel like, but I feel like I've never felt like this before! I feel like I cannot stand to be away from you; I feel like I just want to be with you all of the time. I *love* you too Noam."

And then he kissed me!

Dysmas
(Sunset)

They got me. They finally caught me!

I enjoyed living my life alone, and being alone out in the desert away from the people. People are never happy it seems. They complain about almost everything in their lives. Their work, their wages, their health, their spouse, their children, their aches, their future. It's unending and I for one cannot stand to hear it and fake my interest in their problems.

That's why I don't want to be around them. But I DO like when our paths cross! There isn't much out here in this area I call home. I have access to a water supply, a brick walled adobe that I call home, and I find comfort hiding in the everlasting clouds of chalky dust. Every once in awhile, a small caravan of travelers come near and I will attack them for whatever they may have of value. That is where I get my money from – from *them*.

I regret killing that woman only for the reason that it was her screaming that called the others to me. They found me like a lion finds its prey. They found me because of her constant and unbelievable crying at such a pitch that even I could not suppress it. It was only in her death that she stopped and by then, it was too late for me to escape the men who found us.

The trial was swift and now I am a condemned man. I am to be made an "example of" is what the judge had said. 'You will be put to death by crucifixion' he said and now I find myself in this god-forsaken prison. It smells and is filled with men of all shapes, sizes, and convictions. Of course, they are filled with complaints. 'I was wrongly convicted', 'I am innocent', 'I didn't do it', are some of the constant cries I hear from these feeble-minded criminals. I can't stand it. There should be no hiding if you are guilty. God sees. God knows. This is why I hate people; no accountability, and no responsibility! But God knows! There is NO hiding from Him!

This prison reeks of the smells of strife, stress and the excrement of too many people shoved into too small of a place. My cell is crammed with 25 men when there is room for only half of that. The judgement for all of us has been made and we wait for our final judgement by the Lord our God.

I know what you are thinking. If I fear God, why then did I do what I did without mercy? The flesh is weak, as am I. I have waited for God to find ME. Why did He not find me?

Just then one of the Roman guards calls out "Listen here you slobs! Anyone who would like to see a priest, please step forward. Not that it will help any of you pigs!" as he laughed at all of us jammed into the cell block.

I needed to get away from this cell so I anxiously stepped forward. "I would like to se a priest" I said to the guard. Just a few more also said they would like to see a priest. The rest just grumbled and complained. Of course, they did. People, ugh!

They led us to another area within the prison. It looked like an old cave but a very large one at that. The ceiling height was about 12 feet tall and the width was about 30 feet wide. There were ledges all around which made it appear as if they were benches carved out of the stone. The walls had lanterns which provided some light and the air was cool. It was a cleaner air too without the smell of urine and sweat. A nice change for sure.

There was only one way in and one way out which is heavily guarded by 6-7 soldiers. Maybe they were there to protect the priest because there certainly was no way to escape from this cave, never mind the prison.

"Please be seated" said the priest as he occupied the highest of the stone ledges within the cave. "Your fate awaits you within the next several days and you are all sentenced to death so I am told."

Most of us simply bowed and kept our gazes towards the rock floor. One man began to weep. The priest began to read from the Torah, a blessing I think, to calm all of us.

I find myself thinking about human nature and humility. When we finally surrender ourselves and recognize that we truly have limited control over our own destiny, we become different. We realize that we have no power over most things and that we are not in control. We sort of fade into the background and any aggression that we may possess is gone. What are we at this point then? The only thing I can think of is we are dependent on someone or something else.

I look up at the priest and he is reading to us Psalm 51 which apparently is a prayer for mercy and pardon. He reads,

"Wash away all my iniquity and cleanse me from my sin. For I know my transgressions, and my sin is always before me. Against you, you only, have I sinned and done what is evil in your sight......" (Psalm 51:2-4) As he continues to read, I find my mind going to another place within my thoughts. His voice is hypnotic and yet calming and I find myself thinking about that I haven't thought about in a long, long time; God.

In this moment of humility, I actually find myself as a disappointment to Him. I have built this structure, a defensive wall that somehow, now in this moment, has been torn down. I am nothing. All that I am has been a self-motivated power grab seeking things of a world that will have no meaning after I am dead. There is NO power in that. There is no power in taking things away from people when I should be doing the exact opposite – giving to them instead!

"Create in me a pure heart, O' God" I hear the priest reading *"and renew a steadfast spirit within me. Do not cast me from your presence or take your Holy Spirit from me. Restore to me the joy of your salvation and grant me a willing spirit to sustain me."* (Psalm 51:10-12)

Is it possible to return to God when you have rejected Him? Has He forgotten me because I am evil and have done so many evil things? Would He take back a sinner like me? Am I like one of those who killed children of God in the Valley of Gehenna?[1] I need to be destroyed because I have done nothing with my life? My thoughts are running rapidly through my mind when I hear the priest ask if there is anyone who would like to confess their sins at this time in our gathering. I feel that he has directed that question to me; that he can see what's in my mind and what I am thinking! But I am not alone as many others raise their hands too.

In this very moment I have been broken down, I have been humbled. If there is a God for me, I must beg His forgiveness and tell Him of my sorrow and regret for the things I did against Him. I feel the tears streaming down my face as I rise and approach the priest to receive his prayer for me and to confess my sins. I am lost. Will God find me still?

---

[1] Gehenna was the valley of Hinnom located just below Jerusalem. It was here that renegade Jews sacrificed their children to the pagan god Moloch. Later it became a place for refuse to be incinerated.

Noam
(Tenderness)

Ever since that first kiss, I have spent as much time as I can with Talia. Thankfully, both of our parents have been in "preparation mode" getting things ready for the seder meal and all that goes into the festivities of this week, so we have been out of their sights, for the most part that is.

There is a nice breeze here as we are sitting under the olive tree. The sun is high in the sky and there is much traffic on the Bethany Trail, as it is known. The foot traffic seems to be rather heavy today and actually heading away from Jerusalem. I am wondering why that is because that seems contrary in light of the upcoming events.

"So, Talia, tell me about where the Paschal lamb comes from again."

"Well Noam, of course you know that the Paschal lamb is the Passover lamb. This *perfect* lamb is sacrificed on the evening of Passover according to the rules of the Torah. Remember that the blood of a lamb was used to mark the Jewish residences to save them from the angel of death? And then Pharoah let them escape out of Egypt?"

"Yes, Talia. Of course, I remember *that*!"

"Well, the Paschal lamb actually comes from the area of Bethany up east of here."

"Fascinating, simply fascinating Talia. And I needed to know that because?"

"Oh Noam, you make me laugh! I just thought it was interesting because rumor has it that Jesus in actually up in Bethany."

"Really? Now how did you hear of this?"

"People in the markets and on the streets. Everyone here in Jerusalem has heard of all of the things that Jesus has done and they seem to know where and what he says and does. His words and actions get around pretty quickly in these parts. Most still have never seen him here. From what I hear, he will be here for the Passover festival again this year."

"Talia, have you noticed all of these people walking by us here today? They are walking *away* from the markets and, well, heading in the direction of Bethany and *not* Jerusalem?"

And just in that moment I see Nathaniel walking in front of us heading east towards Bethany!

"Hey Nathaniel! Nathaniel! Over here!" I'm waving at him with both of my arms. "Over here Nathaniel!"

Finally, he stops as he hears his name being called. He looks around to see where the sound is coming from – ah yes, he sees me now.

"Hey, Noam! Hi Talia! What a coincidence running into you here! You know, with the crowds and all that, it's amazing to run into anyone you might know! How are you both? Are you going to Bethany too?"

"Ok, ok, exactly *what's* happening in Bethany anyway? We see all of these people heading that way but we don't know why! What are they going to escort the Paschal lamb or something like that?" I asked sarcastically.

"You mean you guys haven't heard of the miracle Jesus performed? Raising Lazarus from the dead?"

"WHAT?" I can't believe what I am hearing! I look over to Talia and she too has a look of astonishment on her face too!

"Nathaniel, what exactly do you mean 'raised from the dead'"

"Yes, it is true! Come let's go. I'll tell you the story while we walk. We are all going to Bethany because that is where Jesus is right now! It's our chance to be with him!"

Talia and I gathered up our belongings from under that olive tree and joined together with Nathaniel and began our trek towards Bethany.

Nathaniel, Talia and I began our walk and we were pretty excited. Jerusalem was alive and filled with energy and now here we were off to actually have a chance of meeting Jesus. Nathaniel told us that Jesus and he were actually friends and that Jesus would often send him out to deliver many of his messages to the people throughout Galilee.

"Jesus has these close friends of his that live in Bethany. There are actually 3 of them; Martha, Mary, and Lazarus.

So, a little over a week ago, Lazarus became very sick but Jesus had already left and had ventured to the place where John the Baptist began his baptisms" Nathaniel explained. "Well then, Lazarus actually dies from his illness!

Lazarus was very well known and respected within Bethany so everyone was mourning over his death and for Mary and Martha's personal loss."

"The sisters were very upset that Jesus had not returned in time to heal their brother even though they had sent word for Jesus to come back to Bethany very quickly. By the time Jesus made it back to Bethany, Lazarus had been dead for four days!"

Talia looked up to Nathaniel and said "Oh my goodness! How sad is that? But I thought you said that Lazarus is alive?"

I said to Talia "slow down and let him finish this story!" As I looked to the road that lay ahead of us, I couldn't help but notice a large bank of clouds in the sky that were quickly approaching offering us a respite from the hot midday sun. It was welcome for sure as was the improving breeze.

Nathaniel continued. "On the way back to Bethany, some of the disciples that were with him asked Jesus 'you said that Lazarus had fallen asleep, so are we going then to wake him up?'

And then Jesus told them *"Lazarus is dead, and for your sake I am glad I was not there, so that you may believe. But let us go to him."* (John 11:14-15).

"I find this very interesting my friends. Jesus told them that he was glad he wasn't there! He said that he was glad so that they would believe!"

"I'm lost" I said. "The disciples have already seen so much of the powers of Jesus! What more does it take to 'believe' that Jesus is something greater than any of us can imagine?"

Nathaniel continued. "So, Jesus arrived at Bethany, and Lazarus had already been in the tomb for 4 days now. Four days! As you know from our Jewish teachings that when somebody dies, their soul remains in the body for three days. This was day 4; Lazarus was dead, and his soul has moved on!"

"It was Martha who first saw Jesus and she was very upset and emotional. She passionately told Jesus that if he had only been there sooner that she knew he could have saved her brother. However, in her heart, she remained faithful for some miracle to happen. She told Jesus that God would give Jesus whatever it was that he asked." Nathaniel said.

"I think that is so important for all of us to focus upon – faith in our God! Remember when Jesus taught us to pray and he said '*thy Kingdom come, thy will be done*'? Martha had the *faith* that something would come of her brother's death and it would be on God's timing that it would happen. Plus, she told Jesus 'I know he will rise again in the resurrection at the last day'."

"Yes, that is true *faith*!" added Talia. "So, Nathaniel, what happens next? If Lazarus is in the tomb, dead now for four days, the people are mourning, what can Jesus possibly do now?"

Nathaniel stopped walking and looked into our eyes. His face was unreadable but very serious looking and said "The people I know have told me how this happened. They have also told me *what* Jesus said to Martha and those around him.

Jesus said '*Did I not tell you that if you believed, you would see the glory of God?*' '*Father, I thank you that you have heard me. I knew that you always hear me, but I said this for the benefit of the people standing here that they may believe that you sent me. Lazarus come out!*' And then Lazarus walked out of the opened tomb very much alive!"

Talia
(Dew from God)

We continued on our way towards Bethany. The road was getting clogged with pilgrims and our pace was clearly slowing. The road was getting thick with people and somewhere up ahead we could hear the roar of a crowd. We all slowed to the new pace as a hoard of young pilgrims ran past us with the speed of Olympians!

"What is happening?" I began.

People were running while others stopped. Some were running with palm branches in their hands while others were climbing palm trees and pulling the palms off and passed them around. Then, as people stopped, they began laying down the palms while many others took off their robes and cloaks and laid them down.

Nathaniel, the tallest of us three, could see a little farther ahead than we could. "I think I can see something about a half mile up ahead of us. But it's hard to see because there are so many people crowding the road! It's like a parade for someone important, you know, like the Emperor or a King of some other country is coming!"

I looked at Noam and he was jumping up and down in place to try to see what was up ahead of us. Trying to get a vision of what this commotion could possibly be over. "Noam", I said, "stop that jumping! You're only going to exhaust yourself."

"Talia. Let me be. I think I saw something like a cart coming this way."

"No, Noam, I can see it now! It's a man or something on a horse or donkey. And the people are laying down palms and cloaks and robes in its path." said Nathaniel.

And then we heard the cries louder as that thing, whatever it was, was getting closer to us. Wait, wait, I think I can hear it now. Yes, I can hear it clearly now as the people are crying out in unison. "HOSANNA! Blessed is he who comes in the name of the Lord! Blessed is the King of Israel!"

The three of us are astonished and looking at one another with wonder on our faces while the cries of Hosanna are getting louder and louder.

And there he was! Right in front of us riding a donkey with its colt behind it. People laying their palms and robes just as if Jesus was a king. But not a king. A king, a warrior would be riding a great stallion. Jesus is riding a donkey, without a threat, and a sign of peaceful entry.

We too joined the throngs crying out "Hosanna! Hosanna! Blessed is he who come in the name of our Lord!"

I have never seen so many people gathered as Jesus continues his slow trek upon his donkey. Jesus WILL be here for the Passover! There were many that were saying that he wouldn't come this year because of the threats from the priests and their scribes. There were also rumors that they wanted to actually kill him! Can you imagine this coming from our religious leaders? My father better not be a part of that for sure!

Suddenly, there was a loud noise that came from somewhere above us, right where we stood, and we could see that Jesus had stopped his donkey and was also looking up at the sky. It was as if a storm was brewing and thunder was ahead of it. Was it a voice? But we heard words now, but like thunder. Some of the people who were also looking up were saying "Is it an angel?" while others began saying "Is it God that we are hearing?"

The words we heard? *"I have glorified it and I will glorify it again."*

"And then Jesus said, *This voice was for your benefit, not mine. Now is the time for judgment on this world; now the prince of this world will be driven out. But I, when I am lifted up from the earth, will draw all men to myself."* (John 12:30-33)

The three of us, marveling at what just happened and looking towards Jesus, we dropped to our knees and bowed our heads. This was *the* moment I knew that this was the Christ, the Messiah! How could he not be? Our savior has come! Hosanna! Hosanna! Blessed is HE who comes in the name of the Lord!

And then Jesus mounted the donkey and continued on his journey passing the throngs of people joyously shouting out his name and the Hosannas. We have met our King! Hosanna in the highest!

Petronius – The Centurion (Unsophisticated)

Yesterday, I just watched him. I knew this man was Jesus. As I stood on the Temple grounds watching the crowds thin out near the end of the day, I saw him approach the Golden Gate. The money changers were just packing up their tables and the sun was lower in the sky as it was preparing to set on the day.

It was an interesting day watching the throngs of pilgrims moving about Jerusalem and I know our guards were stretched to the limit. From the west came Pilate and his parade of legionnaires and the drum beats and spectacle of his arrival and the hordes of people to witness such a parade.

From the east, yet another crowd lined the street throwing down palms, and robes while Jesus came into the city riding a donkey. The people were cheering and chanting Hosannah almost uncontrollably. I decided that I would follow Jesus' processional as it could become more volatile in nature. It seemed to me that it was more passionate in nature and could get out of hand. A heightened sense of pure excitement I guess one could say.

And now, here he is now at the Temple. Just watching and observing. I sense there is more to it than that however. I sense a sadness about him. I can't really explain it but as he is walking the courts of the Temple, he appears to be disappointed, his shoulders not as upright, his head slightly bowed, his sandaled feet shuffling. I can't help but to think that Jesus sees no improvement to the Temple environment since his last visit three years ago.

I followed him from a fair distance so he did not notice me. No one was with him or followed him. I wondered how he finally was alone like this. All of the people have finally left him to himself? All of the things that I have heard about the crowds that surround him, and he is finally alone? There is a quiet sadness about all of this and I feel there is some type of change that is in the air as I watch him turn and leave the courts.

π

And now today, a new day, and it is totally different! The commotion at the Temple grounds has reached a feverish pitch! There is screaming and yelling and as I run towards the epicenter of the noise and there he is. Jesus. He is overturning the money changers tables with a passion I've not seen from him before. I remember three years ago when he did this same thing, but this time is different. This time is very different as was his reception. It seems like the priests were waiting for this to happen. Again. This time they are ready for him. They have assembled to watch him as if they are scheming for something else.

I can see a different Jesus today. The gentleness is gone and I can feel anger in his actions. The people are yelling and pointing fingers at him while he is shouting about them being robbers and the Temple is the house of God; a place to be respected and not for thieves who take money from His people in His name.

It's usually all about money, isn't it? It begins with the Temple. The Temple has a treasury and it generates income from the various laws they create and impose them upon the people. Some can afford to pay these Temple taxes while others cannot. It is quite common knowledge and practice that the Temple authorities issue loans to those less fortunate who cannot afford to purchase sacrifices nor afford the tax. These loans charge exorbitant interest rates which further exploit the poor and place hardship upon them, all in the name of God.

God is to be the people's protector and moral compass yet here; God has been positioned by the priests as a taker and placing undue hardship upon His people. These Jewish people, the people of the Temple, are an interesting lot for sure. They, in the name of their God, place a heavy price for salvation.

One thing that I have learned about Jerusalem and the Jews, respect and status is solely based upon who you are and your family status. They elevate themselves and look down upon those not in their status class. Their high priest, Joseph Caiaphas, even has his own palace in the Upper City located across the valley from the Temple. He is a powerful man, not well liked, but he has the money to "influence" almost anything he desires.

I have the acute sense that the enemies of Jesus are none other than the Temple aristocracy. Jesus is clearly a threat to the status quo which makes him very unpopular amongst the Temple leaders.

I can't help but be amazed by Jesus' actions. The Temple grounds cover almost 35 acres of buildings and courts and this area called the Court of the Gentiles covers one third of it. It is a very large area and now holds most of the cattle that are used for their sacrifices. Filled with hay, and dust, and excrement from these beasts, it hardly represents what I would think of a holy area. It's more of a pigs-stye in my opinion.

And Jesus, with about 300 of his followers, has upset the entire area! My legionnaires are closely watching them as they methodically overturn tables, and clear out the stables and totally disrupting the affairs at the Temple. My legionnaires stand ready to intervene but these Jesus followers are not breaking any Roman laws so we remain on the peripheral and simply stand firm to keep some sense of order. It is the priests and the scribes who are fumbling about trying to chase Jesus and his followers away.

As I continue my rounds and walk through the court, I see a small assembly of pilgrims gathered in a circle, and on their knees. It is clear that they are praying together. I walk closer so that I can hear what it is that they are praying.

"Come join us centurion." one of them says to me. "Our Lord has come and He is fulfilling what the prophet Isaiah has foretold hundreds of years ago. Come pray with us."

I stood close to their circle but did not break into it. And I did drop to one knee and listened to them.

"Here is my servant whom I have chosen, the one I love, in whom I delight; I will put my spirit on him, and he will proclaim justice to the nations. He will not quarrel or cry out; no one will hear his voice in the streets. A bruised reed he will not break, and a smoldering wick he will not snuff out, till he leads justice to victory. In his name the nations will put their hope." (Matthew 12:18-21)

As I listened to this prayer, I couldn't help but think of Qen, my faithful servant, and my friend. It was Jesus who saved him from his illness and restored his life. It was through my faith that my servant was healed; my faith in Jesus.

It was Jesus who called out to his followers to come to him in faith. Those who were sick, those were troubled, those who were weary, and invited them to come to him. It will be Jesus who will take your yoke and give you the rest your soul needs. He will heal your soul but you must believe in him and his kingdom he speaks of.

I rose back to my feet and felt my mind was awash with so many thoughts.

"Thank you, gentlemen, for inviting me to your prayer" I said to them. They bowed their heads in unison and continued on with their prayers.

I wondered as I began my walk again, *who* is Jesus? So many are declaring that Jesus will be their savior, their king, yet he enters into the city on a donkey, the sign of peaceful intent. He comes to the Temple to preach and he is challenged by the Sanhedrin and the Pharisees often times even accusing him of blasphemy. Then he disturbs the 'business of the Temple' affirming that the place of worship, God's Temple, is simply a house of prayer and *not* a place of business to steal from those who worship God.

Somehow, I feel that the answers are coming soon. The spirit in the air is both joyous and tense. This cannot continue without something significant happening and the Jewish people are definitely choosing sides; to follow tradition or to follow this new message that Jesus is bringing. Salvation is earned or is salvation granted to all of those who simply love and honor God?

"Centurion!" I hear someone calling.

It is one of my legionnaires. "Sir, Pilate has ordered that you return to the fortress immediately."

"Yes of course. I will return with you now."

Dysmas
(Sunset)

I was awoken by the clamoring of the guards and the sounds of a new prisoner being brought into our cell. It was dark and most of the men in our cell simply grumbled as they tried to sleep on the crowded floor. This new prisoner was covered in a blanket of sorts and his face was hidden so it was difficult to tell his condition.

As the guard opened the cell door and shoved this man into our quarters he stated "Have a good rest now until the priests summon you again that is." and the guards all chuckled while others laughed out loud. They were gone as quickly as they arrived.

"Here, come sit by me." I said to the new arrival. "I'll make room for you right here."

Now I could see his face as he shifted and sat next to me on the stone floor. His face was swollen apparently from some type of beating he received. His eyes were almost shut from the swelling and blood dripped from his broken nose. Certainly, he must be in a great deal of pain!

"I wish I could offer you more, but as you can see we have nothing to offer you here in the cell. I'm sorry I can only offer my sympathy for your condition."

He looked at me, and smiled. Not a full smile, but it was a smile of gratitude that I was even willing to offer some type of assistance to him. And then he nodded and closed his eyes in an apparent attempt to rest. Only a few minutes later I felt his body lean against me as I heard a soft snore from him. He did find rest in spite of his injuries.

I began to think of my time with the priest, and his prayers, and my confession earlier this evening. Somehow, I felt closer to God and clean after I confessed my sins. Not some, but all of them. I thought about the strength we can receive from God if we believe in Him. I thought about the strength He gives us and then how we should pass it along to others! We all need Him and we need each other. If you have faith in God, all difficulties can be solved! It's never too late to turn to God!

My thoughts brought such a warming feeling that I felt throughout my whole body! I had never felt anything like this and it actually scared me. What was happening here? I shifted slightly to adjust my body and the man shifted off my shoulder and kind of startled awake.

"Oh I'm so sorry to have awoken you! I just had to move slightly. I'm sorry. Are you Ok?"

"It is no problem, my brother." he said. Is there any water here?"

"No there isn't I'm sorry to say. They usually bring us a cup when the sun arises and that's likely still a few hours away. May I ask your name?"

"Yes you may. My name is Jesus."

I am stunned! This is the man I have heard so much about and here he is! Leaning against me! I'm not sure exactly what I feel however. Awe? Pity? Sadness? I am flushed with emotion and am speechless. He has been battered, almost beyond recognition, yet there is a peace about him. He straightens himself up and leans against the wall at our backs. He looks at me with kind eyes, and smiles ever so slightly.

"Don't be afraid of those who want to kill your body, he says to me, *they cannot touch your soul. Fear only God, who can destroy both soul and body in hell. What is the price of two sparrows – one copper coin? But not a single sparrow can fall to the ground without your father knowing it. And the very hairs on your head are all numbered. So don't be afraid; you are more valuable to God than a whole flock of sparrows."*

This man doesn't even know me and he is speaking to my heart and soul. Inside my body, inside of my heart, I feel his words reaching very deep within me and somehow giving me assurance! I DO matter! I feel loved, which is totally weird because no one loves me! Yet his words and his presence has penetrated the darkness within me.

Everyone who acknowledges me publicly here on earth, I will also acknowledge them before my father in heaven." (Matthew 10:28-32)

Just as Jesus was finishing this last thought, we hear the guards approaching calling out his name.

"Jesus, Jesus, King of the Jews! Here we come to get you! You are needed once again. We are coming to worship you."

They are chuckling and speaking in jest with little respect for this man. Jesus begins to gather himself and stands up on his own as they approach our cell gate. He looks at me once again and smiles at me, ever so softly.

Then another set of guards were coming down the same hallway calling out "Barabbas, Barabbas! Come to the gate of your cell!"

In the back quarter of our crowded cell block I see him standing up and approaching the cell gate where a moment ago I stood with Jesus. He is a strong looking man and appears to be in very good shape; like a kind of warrior or soldier of some sort.

When Barabbas finally pushes forward through the rest of the crowded cell, he calls out "I am here" to the guards. "I am here."

"You are being released you miserable dog!" said the centurion in charge. "By the judgment of Pilate, and the people who cried for your release, you have been selected to be set free."

"You are scum and nothing more than a terrorist, a member of the Sicarri (the dagger-bearers), and you deserve to die for murdering Roman soldiers." As Barabbas was exiting through the cell block door, one of the guards punched Barabbas in the stomach which had the desired intent of knocking the wind out of him collapsing him onto his knees.

"You deserve to die, you bastard." and off they went.

As for me? I sat back down, closed my eyes and began to think of those words Jesus said to me. Don't be afraid of those who want to kill your body he said. They cannot touch your soul. And that I am *valuable!*

A worthless, sinner such as I? How can I be valuable? But somehow, the way he said it to me, I believe him; he thought I WAS valuable. A miserable, forgotten wreck, who offered nothing to this world but woe and misery, may actually be worth something? I am having a hard time understanding this, but somehow, in my heart, I want to believe what he told me.

"Don't be afraid" he told me. How can I not be? Today I will die.

Jacob
(May God Protect)

What has happened? The day began according to our Jewish tradition with the "Feast of Unleavened Bread". The unleavened bread is a reminder to us. When our forefathers fled Egypt, they did not have the time to bake any bread using leaven, which is nothing more than fermented dough. So the" bread" was flat and did not rise without the yeast. Given this history, our people believe that fermentation is equivalent to putrefaction; in other words, the process of decay or rotting within the body. So you see, the leaven, to us, represents all that is rotten and corrupt in this world.

Jesus and his disciples gathered in a place located in the upper room of an inn and began their Seder meal together. Amongst the things offered for the meal, there is a bowl of salt water to remind them of the tears they shed while they were slaves in Egypt. It is also a reminder of the salt waters of the Red Sea that God had parted to enable their escape. There are bitter herbs; a reminder of the bitterness of being a slave. And there are four cups of wine to remind us of the four promises of Exodus 6:6-7. *"I will free you from the burdens of the Egyptians and deliver you from slavery to them. I will redeem you with an outstretched arm and with mighty acts of judgment. I will take you as my people, and I will be your God."*

After their supper, three of them went up to the Mount of Olives to a place known as the Garden Gethsemane. Since Jerusalem sits on top of a hill and there is little room in this city for any noncommercial space, every inch of this vast city has been taken up. However, many of the wealthy citizens have their own gardens as part of their properties and Joseph had allowed Jesus access to this garden. It was at this garden that Jesus went to and prayed.

Meanwhile, the Sanhedrin had had enough of Jesus and decided they wanted to kill him. The Temple guards assembled and went out that evening to find Jesus. By the time they found him, there was quite a crowd that had joined their effort to locate Jesus. As their search continued into the night, it seemed like more like an animal hunt. The group of searchers became more like a mob, like a sick animal frothing about the mouth. Irrational. Frenzied. Dangerous.

And then word came. Jesus was at Gethsemane. Their search would soon be over. While Jesus was praying in the garden, the Temple guards entered and arrested Jesus. There was a little scuffle but Jesus rebuked Peter to put his sword down and let the arrest continue. Jesus was then taken to the Hall of Hewn Stone and placed before the court of the Sanhedrin. It was night time which is unusual for such a trial to be conducted. They were desperate.

There are 71 members of the Sanhedrin which is comprised of scribes, Pharisees, Sadducees and Temple elders. I am told they were in a murderess mood and wanted a quick trial and wanted Jesus to be put to death. But the law is the law and they needed 23 votes in order to declare Jesus was guilty.

Their problem however, was they needed something to charge Jesus *with*. According to the law, any evidence of wrong-doing must be supported and guaranteed by a minimum of two witnesses. These two witnesses had to be separately examined and they could not have any contact with each other in order to collaborate their stories. As the night went on, the Sanhedrin was failing at this requirement and they were getting very frustrated. They knew what they wanted but could not find a path to their end.

Finally, and totally exasperated, the chief priest, Joseph Caiaphas who was presiding over this scam "trial" asked Jesus "Are you the Messiah? Do you claim to be the Son of God?" At this point, not having anything to charge Jesus with, Jesus could have simply said "no" and the Sanhedrin would have had to let him go at this point. They had nothing to convict him of.

Jesus, such a smart young boy, who grew into a wonderful and faithful man. He loved the Lord, spoke of God's plans and desires for us. He then went out into the world and told the people about God's mercies and loving grace, and healed and taught so many about a new kingdom. His words and actions were all foretold in prophesy and now these religious leaders want him to be killed! In this very moment, all Jesus had to say was "no". But he didn't.

There Jesus stood and looked at the council. He looked at each one of the members, scanning the audience of his accusers, and said "Yes".

Not only did Jesus reply "yes" to the high priest's question, Jesus then recited Daniel 7:13. *"In my vision at night I looked, and there before me was one like a son of man, coming with the clouds of heaven. He approached the Ancient of Days and was led into his presence. He was given authority, glory and sovereign power; all peoples, nations, and men of every language worshipped him. His dominion is an everlasting dominion that will not pass away, and his kingdom is one that will never be destroyed."*

That was it. Most of the Sanhedrin jumped to their feet and cried out "blasphemy" and began spitting on him and hitting him in their outrage. They had their man and they wanted nothing less now than to put him to death.

However, their next problem lay with Roman rule. Only a Roman governor could pronounce a death penalty of which also must be carried out by the Roman authorities. They needed Pilate to carry out the sentencing and the execution of Jesus. They needed charges that Pilate would believe and accept in order for Jesus to be put to death. What would those charges be?

Well, they came up with three. The first being was that Jesus was a revolutionary, the next charge was that Jesus was telling people not to pay their taxes, and finally that Jesus was claiming to be a king.

As I sit here, just inside the Temple's Huldah gates, and watch the crowds still moving throughout the Temple courtyards, I cannot believe what has happened in just a short amount of time. I am not sure that most have even heard of the arrest of Jesus, but the trial will be tomorrow. Jesus will be put before Pontius Pilate to be tried.

This man is an innocent man. He is a good man. Most of us are just beginning to understand the messages and teachings and others are disappointed. Why disappointed? They think and want him to be a king. A king that should have ridden a stallion into Jerusalem, not a donkey. A king who will bring his army in to destroy the Romans and anyone else who will oppress us. A king who will take away all hardships of the downtrodden and bestow riches upon us all. However, this king Jesus, he speaks in parables and talks of things that we cannot see. This king asks for our faith in him and gives us nothing but words.

I must go now. I must get some rest and return tomorrow for this trial. Somehow, I feel it deep into my bones, things are quickly spiraling out of control and this does not bode well for Jesus. I pray that God will be with him.

Pontius Pilate
(Skilled with a Javelin)

"Sir, you have visitors."

"Are they on my schedule for today?"

"No sir, they are not. However, they seem quite agitated and demanded an audience."

"Did they now? Let me guess, it's an assembly of those Jewish priests and scribes? They never stop. It's *always* something with them! Send them in."

In they marched. Ten of them. I knew Jairus, Caiaphas, and Levi but not the others. They introduced themselves as Annas, Shemesh, Dathaes, Gamaliel, Judas, Napthali and Alexander. All dressed in their priestly robes and some dressed as scribes accordingly.

"Gentlemen, please take a seat. So what is happening at your Temple that I should be blessed to have you request this meeting with *me?* I am sure that you are all very busy as we approach your Passover festival!"

It was the chief priest Caiaphas who spoke first. "We are here to request that Jesus be brought here, and to be seated at your seat of judgment in order that he face trial before you."

"Is that so? And exactly what would be the reason I should bring him before me?"

Caiaphas still standing before Pilate, slightly raising his voice and shook his right hand in the air saying "Jesus claims that he is a king and the Son of God!" The other priests and scribes began to grumble and shout out "blasphemy" at this. Caiaphas continued, "He desecrates the Sabbath and wants to overthrow the Laws of Moses! He practices evil deeds and often on the Sabbath day which is against our laws! He is a sorcerer who can cast out demons, he has healed the lame, the withered, the blind, the paralyzed, all in the name of God!"

As I looked around at them, I could tell now that Caiaphas was red in the face and his cheeks were shaking with rage. The others were coming out of their seats with this inflamed passion now running through my audience.

I then stood to reassert my authority and stated "I believe that these actions and healings are accomplished by the divine Asclepius.[2] Tell me then how a mere Governor can accuse a "king" of such things?"

"No, we are not saying he is a king, only that he claims to be one." replied Annas.

"Ok then, I will summon Jesus from the Praetorium of the palace and I will question him." I looked at my courier and told him to get Jesus and to bring him to this assembly.

---

[2] Asclepius is the Greco-Roman god of medicine who has the skill for healing.

When Jesus was brought into their assembly by the standard-bearers holding the ensigns, the emblems of the emperor on them, all but the priests and scribes and I, bowed down to Jesus. Of course, this infuriated the Jews from the Temple.

After calming the court, I then asked Jesus "Why are these people making accusations against you?"

Jesus said *"Unless they had authority, they would not have said anything. For each person has authority over his mouth to speak good or evil. They will see."*[3]

So I asked the priests, "What reason do you want Jesus put to death? Because he healed on the Sabbath? Because he actually did good things?"

In unison, incredibly, they all said "yes".

"I have the sun as my witness" I said, "that I find this man Not Guilty! You take him, then, judge him by your own law!"

"We do not have the authority to execute him under Roman law!"

Jesus looked at me and says to me *"My kingdom is not from this world. If it were from this world, my servants would have struggled against my being handed over to the Jews. So then my kingdom is not from here. You say I am a king. The reason I was born and have come is so that everyone who belongs to the truth should hear my voice. The truth is from heaven. You can see how those who speak the truth are judged by those with earthly authority."*[4]

---

[3] Some excerpts and quotes taken from the Apocryphal Gospels. This one from The Gospel of Nicodemus

I then asked where Jesus was living before he came to Jerusalem.

It was Annas who replied "He resided in Galilee."

"Well then gentlemen, that places him out of my jurisdiction. Your plea to have him tried falls upon Herod Antipas because Galilee is in his district. You all may leave me now. Good day."

The priests then took him over to visit with Herod as he too was in Jerusalem for the festivities. Herod was actually thrilled to have a meeting with Jesus because he wanted to see some of his "magic".

When they arrived, Herod had Jesus dressed in an elaborate purple robe and had him brought into his court surrounded by Herod's soldiers. It was so disrespectful to have a man put into a king's robe and so condescending. Then they spent time hurling insults at Jesus and mocked him while Jesus stood there in front of them. Jesus said nothing and just starred at Herod.

"Show us a few of your tricks Jesus!" Herod said. "Maybe you can make us all blind! Or heal this sore on my foot?"

When Jesus stood there, just starring at Herod, and was unresponsive to any of their insults, Herod became flustered and angry.

---

[4] The Gospel of Nicodemus

"You have nothing to say?" Herod yelled. "No magic for me?" Herod clearly thought Jesus was a joke and did not take him seriously and was frustrated that Jesus would not even respond to any of his taunting. Herod sat there thinking looking at Jesus and was getting more and more agitated due to the lack of Jesus' response.

"Send him back to Pilate! This is nothing I want anything to do with. This man is absurd and get him out of my court right now!"

Here I am again and I am not happy to see the priests nor hearing that Herod wanted nothing to do with any trial of Jesus. Here they all are and I'm feeling like I am trapped. If I didn't do what they wanted they would complain to Tiberius and he would likely have me removed from my office. I am caught in this vice and they are slowly squeezing me into a position with few choices!

I then stood up before this audience and I motioned to the priests to follow me. I left Jesus there and I directed the elders, the priests and the Levites to a secret conference area.

"Do not pursue this! What I have heard from you tells me there is nothing of which you have accused him merits the death penalty. Your only charges against him are defiling the Sabbath and healing on your sacred day. Is this the best you can come up with?"

"If someone were to blaspheme Caesar," they said, would he be worthy of death or not?"

"He would indeed" I stated.

"Well then, whoever blasphemes Caesar merits the death penalty – and Jesus has blasphemed God!

Nicodemus now stood and asked "O venerable governor, may I be permitted to speak briefly?"

"Permission granted."

"This is what I have said to the elders, the priests and the Levites – and indeed to the whole Jewish assembly in the synagogue: 'What do you want with this man? He has performed many miracles and wonders – as no one has done before or could do in the future. Let him go and do not contrive any evil against him. If the miracles he performs are from God, they will stand the test of time, but if they are just human trickery, they will come to nothing. For Moses was sent from God to Egypt and performed many miracles which God had instructed him to do in front of Pharoah king of Egypt. There Pharoah had two servants, Jannes and Jambres, and they too performed a number of miracles which Moses had done. But since these miracles which they performed were not from God, Jannes and Jambres as well as those who believed in them perished. Therefore, let this man go. He does not deserve to die.'"[5]

The Jews were furious at Nicodemus.

"Nicodemus, you can have the truth of that Jesus – and his destiny with it!" they shouted!

---

[5] The Gospel of Nicodemus

Then, several Jews in attendance stood and presented their testimony regarding Jesus. One man had been paralyzed for 38 years and had been healed by Jesus. Another spoke of being healed from disease. Another of being possessed by evil spirits. Another who was blind at birth, and a woman who had a flow of blood for many years. All had been healed by Jesus.

I then called Nicodemus and the ten priests and scribes to me. "What am I going to do here? There is dissent among the people." They simply shrugged and stared back at me. I then called the whole assembly back together again.

"You know that there is a custom at the Passover of one of your prisoners being released. I have a condemned criminal in the prison, a murderer called Barabbas, but this Jesus in front of you here I cannot find guilty of anything. Whom do you want me to release to you?"

"Barabbas! "They shouted.

"What shall I do with this Jesus who is called the Christ?"

"Crucify him!" Said the Jews to the governor. "You are no friend of Caesar if you release this man", some of the Jews added, "because he claims to be a king and a son of God. If you let him go, you would be choosing him as king rather than Caesar."

"We know that Caesar, not Jesus, is king. Certainly, those Magi brought him gifts from the east as if he were a king. But when Herod heard from these Magi that a king had been born, he tried to kill Jesus. When Joseph, his father found out, he took Jesus and the child's mother and escaped to Egypt. Hearing this, Herod killed the children of the Hebrews who had been born in Bethlehem."

"So this is the one Herod pursued?"

"Yes", the Jews said, "this is the one."[6]

I was quickly losing control of the audience and their fervor was accelerating. Capitulating, I took some water and washed my hands. I looked up to the sun and said *"I am innocent of the blood of this righteous man. This is your concern."*

I looked to Jesus and said "Your people have convicted you of being a king. That is why I make my judgment: you are first to be flogged according to the decree of the pious emperors, and then hanged on a cross in the garden where you were arrested, with the criminals Dysmas and Gestas crucified alongside you."[7]

One of my scribes handed me a note as I was finishing my judgment. I opened the note. It was from my wife. It read: 'Have nothing to do with this righteous man, for I suffered terribly because of him last night.'

---

[6] The Gospel of Nicodemus

[7] The Gospel of Nicodemus

As I look at the audience assembled here, I know this man is innocent and the charges against him do not warrant a crucifixion! I'm in a bind here and I do not want the Jews to riot and turn against me again. I see only one way through this craziness and that is to fulfill the will of these people.

I cannot wait until this festival is over and return to my home on the sea. These people bring me nothing but anxiety and I cannot wait to leave them and this crowded city. I dread when the news reaches Tiberius. This is not going to end well.

"Petronius, come to me!" Petronius, who is standing off to the side watching the Jews and their inflamed tempers, immediately comes to my side.

I reached down and grabbed the poster card that gets affixed to the top of the crucifixion cross and began writing. I wrote "Jesus of Nazareth – the King of the Jews". I will hurl such an insult at these Temple leaders for their intimidation and disrespect of me. I know that they hate the Nazarenes and adding further insult by calling Jesus "The King of the Jews"! Then I held up the card and showed it to them. A smile deep in my heart. I loved their reaction!

They all erupted into shouts and cries "NO! You cannot use this inscription! No! Change it to read 'I am the King of the Jews".

I just smiled and waved it in front of their faces.

"People, people, calm yourselves! Do you need to be reminded this was one of your own charges against this man?" That certainly quieted them down! I looked at them all and said "What I have written, is what I have written! Now leave me, I have other business to conduct."

"Petronius, I am appointing you and your legion to lead the procession of Jesus and the two criminals. Here is the poster for the cross of Jesus to be hung for all to see. Be gone with you now."

Noam
(Tenderness)

I cannot hear all that the priests and Pilate are saying but the priests are certainly making their voices heard to Pilate. I can see that a crowd now has gathered around this hearing; well, I guess this is more of a trial so I am told. Jesus appears to be calm and the priests look very agitated!

I have learned about a man named Barabbas, who is in the prison here in Jerusalem. Many people who have joined the growing crowd keep mentioning his name. I hear them as they walk by me. "We must free Barabbas" "We must shout together as one" "Barabbas in one of us – we must save him!" They whisper his name but they all seem to have the same idea. They want him released from prison and his death sentence.

Apparently, this Barabbas is a member of the "dagger-men" who are fanatical nationalists. They are also known as the "sicarii", named after the sicae dagger. They basically are assassins who want to overthrow the Romans and establish an independent Jewish state.

The sicarii's technique was to attend the larger public gatherings hiding their sicaes in their cloaks and garments. At various times within these gatherings, they would attack the Romans and Roman sympathizers by stabbing their targets and quietly blend into the crowd escaping detection. They were trouble makers hoping that their actions would incite a revolution among the people against the Romans.

From what I have heard here, Barabbas is one of them, an insurrectionist. And a very popular one at that! His activities among the sicarii are well known and his actions earned him a very strong reputation amongst these nationalists. However, he was caught by the Romans and has been placed on death row and scheduled to be crucified along with a few others.

Now, from where I am seated, looking down into this crowd, they are chanting "Barabbas, Barabbas, Barabbas".

I see Pilate leaning down from his stage talking with one of the legionnaires. Then the legionnaire runs off towards the prison. The crowd is still chanting "Barabbas, Barabbas" when I see the legionnaire bringing out a prisoner. He is still in chains but they are now removing them. This must be Barabbas. Then Pilate raises both of his arms in the air above his head, and the crowd goes silent. I can now hear Pilate making his decree – "Set this man free, for it is the will of the people!"

It is Pilate's custom, during the Passover festival, to release a single prisoner that the people want to be set free. Based upon what I have witnessed and heard, the largest group here today was made up of predominately nationalists, those who were shouting out "Barabbas". Where were the people who could have saved Jesus? Why weren't they here today? Maybe they didn't know this was being done? Maybe the Temple priests had arranged that his supporters would not know of this trial? That they be kept away?

Suddenly, I see Pilate once again standing up before the crowd, once again with his arms above his head and saying something I cannot hear from where I am. What I hear next burns my ears.

"Crucify him! Crucify him!"

Somehow, I know they are talking about Jesus! Yelling "crucify him", I cannot understand why Jesus is to be put to death! For what did he do? His message was one of hope. His actions were nothing but miraculous. His heart was filled with nothing but love. I cannot believe that this crowd chose a true criminal, a murderer, a law-breaker, a violent man filled with hate over love. All Jesus ever did was give and share love. This is an innocent man!

Where is God? When will He ever bring us salvation into this world filled with sin and hatred? My heart aches and my faith is weak. I was so hopeful that Jesus would be the one for us; our Messiah.

I remember Jesus telling us *"I praise you, Father, Lord of heaven and earth, because you have hidden these things from the wise and learned, and revealed them to little children. Yes, Father, for this was your good pleasure. Come to me, all you who are weary and burdened, and I will give you rest. Take my yoke upon you and learn from me, for I am gentle and humble in heart, and you will find rest for your souls. For my yoke is easy and my burden is light."* (Matthew 11:25-30)

I think about these "wise" priests and Temple leaders who are filled with pride and arrogance and don't understand what Jesus is saying. These *wise* men are in love with themselves and impressed with their own knowledge and are unwilling to learn and understand the message of Jesus. We "children" accept his message because we are faithful, the same as a child.

The message Jesus brings, if we accept it in our heart and soul, can and will relieve us from our burdens of sin and persecution. Our souls can bask in the love, and healing and peace that Jesus gives to us. It is our choice to accept him into our lives. I want that! I accept that! I want to believe!

Petronius – The Centurion (Unsophisticated)

I remember Jesus telling I assembled my troops that next morning at the praetorium just before 9:00am and we collected Jesus. I was shocked to see that he was badly beaten. He had been whipped as well and had stripes across his back that were still bleeding. I have seen many a man whipped and beaten but rarely to this extent.

It is customary that each person who has been sentenced to be crucified is to be accompanied by four Roman soldiers. I selected four of my men and decided that I would also stay with them while we escorted Jesus to Golgotha.

"Lead on soldier – begin our march. Take the direct route to the Damascus Gate this morning. I find little reason to march Jesus throughout Jerusalem." I made certain that I had the inscription with me to post above the head of Jesus. The Jews were very upset how it was written, The King of the Jews, but Pilate was adamant that it remained as he wrote it.

Soon after our march began, the crowds began to swell along the roadway, clogging the dusty streets. It was a warm day already and the sky was filled with sun and big puffy clouds. Actually a very nice day in Jerusalem.

I'm not certain exactly who this crowd was made up of. There were some who jeered and called out insulting comments towards Jesus, I think others were followers of his, and then of course, the curiosity seekers. Nothing like a crucifixion to start one's day! I am thankful that no Roman can be crucified as our laws dictate because this is an awful way to die! Crucifixion is only for criminals and slaves of other countries; never a Roman!

We continued on our way to Golgotha and came upon a group of women who were weeping and beating their chests along the roadside. I slowed our processional down and surveyed the situation for it is against Roman law to show any type of sympathy or emotional outbursts for a criminal on the way to his punishment.

Then Jesus turned toward them and said *"Daughters of Jerusalem, do not weep for me, but weep for yourselves and for your children."* Jesus suddenly stopped and looked directly at their assembly and continued. *"For the days are surely coming when they will say, 'Blessed are the barren, and the wombs that never bore, and the breasts that never nursed.' Then they will begin to say to the mountains, 'Fall on us'; and to the hills, 'cover us'. For if they do this when the wood is green, what will happen when it is dry?"* (Luke 23:27-31)

I think that Jesus maybe be saying that the Jewish people have rejected their prophets from the past and even now they are rejecting him! He compares the green wood to himself and the dry wood is Jerusalem. Is he foretelling of some disaster in the future where there will be much death and destruction?

"Ok men, carry on now! Jesus you must keep moving!"

I stare at these women who are disobeying the law and then have silenced themselves. Thankfully. I do not need any trouble this morning. I have noticed the crowd has grown another ten-fold and we must keep moving. I look again over at Jesus and he is not well at all. He has lost so much blood and the heat is coming upon us already, and looks very, very weak.

Just as I am thinking this he tumbles to the ground. He has dropped the crossbeam and is on his knees, desperately weakened. My four soldiers begin kicking him to get him to stand up and resume his walk.

"Men! Stop kicking him!" I have seen the punishment Jesus has already endured but I cannot show any weakness to my soldiers.

"You there. What is your name?"

"I am Simon of Cyrene. I have done nothing wrong, sir"

"Pick up that crossbeam that he was carrying! You will carry it for him until we reach Golgotha!"

"Sir, I am on my way to the Temple to participate in some of the Temple Passover services. I have traveled from Northern Africa from the city of Cyrene. I do not even know this man!"

"You will do as I say or I will see to it you will spend the rest of this week in prison for disobeying my order!"

I must have gotten through to this Simon of Cyrene because he bent down and picked up the crossbeam that Jesus was carrying. It is custom that the criminal carries the crossbeam to his crucifixion; the pole is transported by our soldiers to the crucifixion sight. They dig the hole for the post to be erected in and wait for the crossbeam to arrive along with the criminal.

Finally, we are here at Golgotha. It is almost 9:30am. My men have begun the process of attaching the crossbeam to the post while others are preparing Jesus, Dysmas, and Gestas for their fate. It is our custom to remove all of their clothing however the Jews are strongly against this tradition so we provide a loin cloth for a Jewish victim.

It is only a few more minutes before the soldiers are finished with their craft, and the three criminals are hoisted up and their crosses are now vertical. They are only about three feet above the ground so they can hear the words people say to them; mostly insults I'd say.

Sure enough, my men (as it is custom) are dividing the criminal's clothing amongst themselves. I begin to watch the team that is handling Jesus' garments. The four soldiers split up the garments as a little extra reward for their duty. I see one takes his sandals, one takes his girdle, another his undershirt, and the other his cloak.

"What is the problem men?"

"Sir, this cloak is seamless and is very unique indeed and has more value than any other of his garments. If we cut it up, then it will be totally without any value at all!"

"You are Roman soldiers! Certainly, you can find a solution to this problem of yours?"

"Yes, sir. I believe we will simply cast lots for it amongst ourselves."

"Very well. You are to stand watch over this crucifixion and make sure there is no trouble from these observers. I will tell the other men to do the same. There must be over 1,000 people here and we mustn't let anything unusual happen here today!"

I looked to the sky and supposed that it was around 11:30am. It's going to be a long day.

Talia
(Dew from God)

I cannot believe that I am here at Golgotha and with the friends and family of Jesus! It was my mother, earlier this week, who introduced them to me. Such beautiful loving souls they all are and so generous as well. Truly I have been blessed to have met them.

And now, on this awful morning, the Roman soldiers are putting Jesus to death! The man who saved my life is giving up his own! He is not guilty of anything and the charges against him are outrageously evil and dishonest.

We are closely gathered here at the foot of the cross. We must be careful not to weep too loudly as it is against Roman law to show any sympathy towards the victims of a crucifixion. We are just ten feet away from him and we can hear his words along with the others who jeer against him. We can also hear the two who are being crucified alongside of Jesus. I wish I could just jump up and save Jesus from this painful death! My heart aches to see this happen!

John, a disciple of Jesus is here with us too. The mother of Jesus, Mary is here. Ruth, Jude (the brother of Jesus), Salome (John's mother) and the sister of Jesus' mother, Mary wife of Clopas. Also, Mary Magdalene is here with us too.

The jeers we hear are senseless and awful. They are yelling to Jesus to save himself if he really is God. They say why doesn't he tear down the Temple and rebuild it in 3 days as he said he would. Others yell he can save others but can't even save himself. Then another jeer is 'Look at our king next to two criminals – what kind of king is that?'

Gestas, the criminal on the left of Jesus began to shout out to Jesus: 'What terrible things I have done on the earth,' he wailed. 'If I had known that you were the king, I would have tried to kill you. Why do you say you are the Son of God, but aren't able to help yourself in a crisis? Or how can you help another person when they pray to you? If you are the Messiah, come down from the cross, and then I'll believe in you! As far as I can see, you're not even a man; you're just a wild animal dying just as I am.' He started saying many other things against Jesus, blaspheming and grinding his teeth at him."[8]

---

[8] Taken from "The Narrative of Joseph of Arimathea

"Dysmas saw the divine grace of Jesus and also shouted out: 'I know, Jesus Christ,' he said, 'that you are the Son of God. I can see you, O Christ, being worshipped by myriads of myriads of angels. Forgive me the sins which I have committed! While I am assessed when you come to judge all the world, do not bring the stars or the moon as witness against me, for I have plotted many evils during the night. Do not call the sun, which is currently darkened because of you, to recount the evils of my heart. For I cannot provide you with any gift for the forgiveness of my sins. Master, before my spirit departs, grant that my sins be washed away, and remember me – though a sinner – in your kingdom, when you sit on your great and highly exalted throne and come to judge the twelve tribes of Israel." [9]

And for all of this, Jesus has said nothing against them! I'm close enough to him that I can hear him saying something softly, over and over again. As I concentrate on what he is saying I recognize it completely! Of course! Jesus is reciting Psalm 22!

At times it's just a whisper and at others it comes out much louder, some almost like a yell. I know he is weak so this must be excruciating for him to do! But I know this Psalm. David wrote it as a prayer during a time of great suffering when he was rejected not only by his friends but from God Himself.

Psalm 22:

---

[9] Taken from "The Narrative of Joseph of Arimathea.

1-3: My God, my God, why have you forsaken me? Why are you so far from saving me, so far from the words of my groaning? O my God, I cry out by day, but you do not answer, by night, and am not silent

6-8: But I am a worm and not a man, scorned by men and despised by the people. All who see mock me; they hurl insults, shaking their heads: He trusts in the Lord; let the Lord rescue him. Let him deliver him, since he delights in him.

11-18: Do not be far from me, for trouble is near and there is no one to help. Many bulls surround me; strong bulls of Basham encircle me. Roaring lions tearing their prey open their mouths wide against me. I am poured out like water, and all my bones are out of joint. My heart has turned to wax; it has melted away within me. My strength is dried up like a potsherd, my tongue sticks to the roof of my mouth; you lay me in the dust of death. Dogs have surrounded me; a band of evil men has encircled me, they have pierced my hands and my feet. I can count all my bones; people stare and gloat over me. They divide my garments among them and cast lots for my clothing.

25-31: From you comes the theme of my praise in the great assembly, before those who fear you will I fulfill my vows. The poor will eat and be satisfied; they who seek the Lord will praise him – may your hearts live forever! All the ends of the earth will remember and turn to the Lord, and all the families of the nations will bow down before him, for dominion belongs to the Lord and he rules over the nations. All the rich of the earth will feast and worship; all who go down to the dust will kneel before him – those who cannot keep themselves alive. Posterity will serve him; future generations will be told about the Lord. They will proclaim his righteousness to a people yet unborn – for he has done it.

Jude asks me "Talia, can you hear him? Even in his distress and suffering he is speaking to God, his father!"

"Jude, what is bringing on this darkness. It's only 1:30pm and yet the sky is getting darker."

At that moment, the criminal hung on the left side of Jesus, Gestas, calls out "Aren't you the Christ? You should save us and yourself if you are really him! Prove to us that you are the Son of Man! End our pain and suffering if it is so! Ha! Just as I have known. There is no Christ and there is no God! You have misled everyone!"

Dysmas, the criminal to the right of Jesus, calls out to Gestas and is telling him to stop. 'We are the criminals you insulant fool and we have received our sentence accordingly. This man has done nothing and certainly does not deserve a death sentence such as our own! Don't you fear God?'"

Then Dysmas looks at Jesus and said "Jesus, will you remember me when you come into your kingdom?"

And Jesus replied to Dysmas *"I assure you that today you will be with me in Paradise."*

As the hours passed, it was now 3 o'clock and the sky was completely blackened. Much of the crowd had now dispersed and either they had lost interest or they were concerned for their own safety. The way the clouds were now swirling, the winds increasing, and the darkness of an inevitable storm, it did indeed become a place you really didn't want to be, but I stayed.

I believe it was right at 3 o'clock when I looked to the cross and saw Jesus look to the heavens and he cried out in one final gasp *"It is finished. Father into your hands I commend my spirit."* And that was it; Jesus no longer suffered. He was dead.

I don't know what I feel. Of course it was awful to be a witness to this, but somehow my heart expected some type of miracle to occur. I mean he healed people, he made the blind see again, the lame walk, he chased the evil spirits from men, he walked on water, why he even promised us a new kingdom! And there he is, lifeless. My goodness he even brought me back to life and Lazarus too. And this is how it ends? Jesus dies just like the rest of us?

Something catches my eye and I turn my head to see about 13 soldiers approaching me. What is happening now?

"Stand aside woman!" one of the soldiers orders me.

"Yes, yes of course. What are you here for?"

"We have been ordered by Pilate to hurry this execution." and he looks at the other soldiers in his company and they begin to chuckle.

"Apparently little girl, your big Jewish leaders believe that it's bad for business to have a Jew being crucified and still alive on the Sabbath. So your Temple leadership asked Pilate if he would have the legs of Jesus broken to expedite his death. We've been ordered to do just that. Now step aside!"

First the soldiers broke the legs of Gestas, and then they moved over to Dysmas and broke his legs. Then they approached where Jesus hung.

"But Jesus is already dead! See, he is not breathing anymore and his body is lifeless! Leave him be!"

The next thing I know, one of the soldiers raised his spear and dug it into Jesus' left side – where his heart would be – and blood and water came out! Could it be Jesus' last message to us? The message is the blood from his body represents redemption while the water that came out at the same time imparts life? I don't know but maybe?

Dysmas
(Sunset)

I see them approaching, the soldiers. I think I know what they are coming here to do. They are coming to break our legs, to speed up our death. I'm in such pain I am thankful for the relief if it is so.

I cannot help but reflect on my life – a wasted life at that. I am a perpetual sinner and I am dying right next to a perfect man. What will happen after my last breath is taken?

Is this it? Is this what life is all about? You live it until you die and that's it? Is there really a God? Will this God take me into His heaven or am I just too big of a sinner? It's awful to think that this is all there is. Life without hope, without love, without compassion, without something bigger. I know I don't qualify for anything other but a life in Hell, but what about Jesus. He said he was on his way to Paradise – and he would meet me there!

That is a good thought and I hope that it is true! We all need to be rescued from our sins. We all make mistakes, but will we get a second chance? A third? To live my miserable life and simply die – there has to be more! Please God, if you are real, can you still save me? My life is almost over, and I am lost and a sinner.

I pray that this is *not* the end so I turn my face to you God, God my Father in heaven, I am lost but I can still be found. Will you find me? I am actually praying, and I hope for your salvation, and your forgiveness. I am dirt, but will you still have mercy upon my soul? Please forgive me, I am ready to receive You! Will you accept me as I am?

Jacob
(May God Protect)

I could not go to Golgotha! I could not bear to see Jesus hung up on a cross! He did not deserve any of this. He is a victim of powerful people that were afraid for themselves and the influence they believe they have. This is such sinful behavior against what God wants for us!

I went instead to the Temple. I thought I might find some kind of peace if I could pray and focus on God's plan for all of us. Somehow this must be a part of His plan, but I'm having a hard time understanding how this could be a part of it. To have His son crucified?

My walk here was uneventful surprisingly enough. I figured there would be so much commotion on the streets but it was nothing more than the usual pulse within Jerusalem. It was a beautiful day however; nicer than many of this past week. The air was clear, clouds darting across the sky, and the sun shining brightly.

However, a strange thing began in the early afternoon. It was getting darker. The sun was being covered up with large, puffy clouds; storm clouds. The day was still warm and comfortable so I just continued with my meditations.

I think it was around 2-3 o'clock; I couldn't see the sun to be totally accurate in its position so my time may be slightly off. But it was really getting dark! It was too early in the day for this kind of darkness. I decided to walk further onto the Temple grounds towards the Hall of the Israelites.

I was reminded how exclusive the Temple leaders have made our religion as I approached the Soreg fence made of large rocks forming a wall of separation. This is where the gentiles were forbidden to enter and were not allowed to go past this fence. Is this really what our God wants? A wall that separates us? The messages that I have heard Jesus speak of is God is for everyone! Not just a few! It seems to me that *all* of the people want a God in their lives; that He is just not for a few. It is easy to see too, we all *need* God in our lives!

As I continued towards the gate, I saw the sign at its entry. A sign that I have seen probably 100 times or more. Today, I feel I am seeing it for the very first time. I am seeing it with fresh eyes. I am seeing it with an open heart. And my heart hurts. The sign says: "No Gentiles Past This Point Under the Penalty of Death". Death? Gentiles are not welcome to worship God? In His house? What have we done Lord?

Isn't real religion supposed to draw strength from God in order to give it to others? We receive God and His blessings upon us in order that we can give it to others in His name! Yes. Yes.

I kept walking. The sky darkening even more.

"What is happening today?" I found myself saying out loud.

I began to see the rest of the Temple grounds with those same new eyes. There was even more separation. There is the Leper Chambers, for those who have been healed of that awful disease. There is another chamber for the Nazerites, and a different chamber just for the women; the Court of Women they call it. It was very impressive however. The gate to enter the Court of Women was constructed of Corinthian brass so large and thick that it took 20 men to open it! This massive piece of art and functionality was yet another example of separating people from people and people from God. Twenty men just to open the doors? And this was as far as the women could go into the Temple. No further could they go or they would face punishment.

I continued down through the Nicanor Gate onto my final destination where I would say my last few prayers at the Hall of the Israelites. It was almost too dark to see anymore! And then I felt the earth tremor! What is this? An earthquake? Definitely, the earth at my feet began to rumble and shake! The Temple walls were making a groaning sound as they appeared to sway back and forth!

I looked over towards the Middle Wall of Partition (another means to separate us) and sat on a stone bench nearest to me. The darkness, the rumbling, the earth shaking at my feet was something I never felt before this moment in my entire life.

For some reason, I thought of Ezekiel the prophet, and his time when it was the Jews who were exiled in Babylon. They were the ones who were separated and discriminated against. It was God through him who said: *I will give you a new heart and put a new spirit in you; I will remove from you your heart of stone and give you a heart of flesh. And I will put my Spirit in you and move you to follow my decrees and be careful to keep my laws. You will live in the land I gave your forefathers; you will be my people, and I will be your God.* (Ezekiel 36:26-28)

By now, the Temple grounds were bound in terror. The priests and laymen were running through the courts trying to escape and yelling out to all in panic. I could not grasp what route to take, or what direction to run in or if I should even move. It didn't appear that any of the buildings would collapse, or the earth would open under our feet, so it seemed senseless to run against or from an unseen enemy. But I did stand and looked towards the Inner Court of the Temple.

"That's strange" I said out loud, more to myself than anyone in particular. The Temple doors were cast open which I have never seen before! They are never open! Are we being attacked? Yet I see no soldiers or enemies nearby. I decided to go towards the gates and peer into the Inner Court.

Oh my! I had never seen the entrance to the Holy Place – only a Priest can enter the Inner Court to see this absolutely amazing (and beautiful) veil! It was almost too much for my mind to comprehend. The multitude of colors woven into the fabric was unbelievable and indescribable. Nothing could ever compare to this!

This veil was at least 50-60 feet tall and was so thick and heavy, just as I have been told. Only a high priest could pass through this veil on his way to the Holy Place, and only once per year, who would then make atonement for all of the sins of Israel. This is the veil behind which the Spirit of God dwelt. It is so massive. We are told that it represents that approaching God is extremely difficult for a sinful man, and that only a high priest could pass through such a huge and heavy veil. He was the only one who could meet with God.

I nearly jumped out of my own skin at that exact moment! I had to immediately cover my ears with the palms of my hands, and I crouched low due to the noise that echoed from beyond the Holy Place, the Holy of Holies, as I watched that magnificent veil completely tear in half! It was tearing from the top to the bottom! What force could make this happen? This fabric wall that separated God from His people, all of the people, has been destroyed! Who did this? Who has this kind of power? What is happening? Why is this happening?

Petronius – The Centurion (Unsophisticated)

A crucifixion is not something to be relished and certainly is not entertainment. Two of the three up on their crosses were criminals. The third man? It was Jesus and surely, he is innocent. It is not my role to judge what my commander orders, but Jesus is innocent. This is not an easy thing to witness.

I remembered my very first encounter with him. I sought him out in the hopes if he was who they said he was, then he could save my servant. And Jesus told me – it is because of your faith, your servant is healed. My faith? I'm just a soldier. What faith do I have in God? When I see this injustice being done here on that cross? When I see men conspire to kill other men? When I see the ravages of war and how the people suffer in their losses? God? Where is the faith for those people?

Well, I suppose if there is a God, then this man Jesus has come very close to it! He was the one who sought out sinners. He was the one who accepted the people who are unacceptable to most. He was the one who healed the incurable; loved the unlovable; gave hope to the hopeless; calmed the storms; fed the 5,000 and then again 4,000 more. Who is this man Jesus?

I watched men vie for the clothes that Jesus wore and then even drew lots because of its potential wealth. I saw them earlier today jamming a crown of thorns onto his head and mocking him as they yelled "Hail, King of the Jews". I saw his back stripped raw from the flogging he took and then how he was so weak from the loss of blood that someone else had to carry his crossbeam.

On that cross I heard him cry out *"My God, My God, why have you forsaken me?"*. I heard him tell the criminal on his right that *"today you will be with me in paradise"* and then I heard him say *"It is finished"*. His final words – what did he mean by that? Soon after, Pilate had ordered more soldiers to Golgotha to expedite his death by breaking his legs. They were too late though; he was already dead.

Then it happened!

The earth began to tremble and shake; clearly an earthquake! Already the sky was black and darkness was upon us and then that tearing sound? What was that? It sounded like a thousand voices screaming. But not really a scream because it wasn't made by humans. It sounded different. Almost like cloth being ripped in half. But where would something like that happen and why could we hear it all the way up on this dreadful hill?

(Matthew 27:51-6) "And, look you, the veil of the Temple was rent in two from top to bottom, and the earth was shaken, and the rocks were split, and the tombs were opened, and the bodies of many of God's dedicated ones were raised, and they came out of the tombs, after his resurrection and came into the holy city and appeared to many. The centurion and those who were watching Jesus with him saw the earthquake and the things that had happened and they were exceedingly afraid. 'Truly', they said,'this man was the Son of God'".

I looked up to Jesus, hanging on that cross, and knew this wasn't an ordinary man. These events seemed to me to be like it was all preordained to happen. Nothing was just. But it happened according to a plan, made somewhere, for some purpose. As I saw the skies begin to clear, and the earth calming, I found my heart putting words into my mouth, and I stood and proclaimed to all those around me, "It's really true; this man was righteous. This was certainly God's Son".

Things like this, the buildup to this day and its conclusion is beyond explanations. This entire thing is based upon faith! Built upon FAITH! And victory comes to those who never let go of their faith and know that God has not forgotten them! It was Jesus who said *"I, when I am lifted up from the earth, will draw all people to myself."* (John:12:32)

Noam
(Tenderness)

It was over. Jesus had died. The dark skies cleared away. The earthquake had subsided. The Temple veil was torn in half. The people returned to their lives. Just an interesting day, a little from the ordinary, and back to the usual cropping of a day. Really? This is it?

Jesus died just like any other man. There were no angels coming to the rescue! None of God's armies came swooping down to save His Son! Maybe those Leaders were right – if you are God, then come down off that cross, they said. He died. Just like Gestas and Dysmas. They all died.

"Hey there Noam! Noam! Come with us, would you? We could use your help!"

I looked up to see Joseph of Arimathea, and Nicodemus walking towards me. They were walking at a rather quick pace, like they were on a mission of sorts. I could see that Nicodemus was carrying quite a large satchel; I could tell he was pretty much struggling with the weight of it.

"Here son, help me carry one of these two satchels – would you take one for me?" Nicodemus dropped both satchels to the ground and then handed me one of them.

"My goodness Nicodemus, this satchel must weigh 30 pounds! What is in it?"

"Noam, it's spices that we will use for the burial of Jesus. We could use your help in preparing Jesus for his burial; will you come with us? Joseph has arranged it with Pilate so we can take the body of Jesus and place him in a tomb that Joseph already has. No one has ever used this tomb before and it is there we will lay the body of Jesus. We could use another set of hands."

"I would be honored to assist you!" So I picked up one of the bags and we all began our walk to the crypt that Joseph had purchased.

None of us spoke all that much on our walk to the tomb. I suppose we were all still numb from the shock of the loss of our friend Jesus. I wondered if Joseph and Nicodemus had their doubts too as to who Jesus really was. I mean we all wanted to believe that Jesus was the Christ, was the Messiah, but why then did he actually die?

"It's just up ahead", said Joseph. "I have also packed fresh linen strips that we can wrap his body in."

Suddenly, Joseph stopped walking and turned to look at Nicodemus and I. He dropped the bag containing the linen strips and he just stood there and starred at us for a minute or two. Finally, he began to speak.

"I am so embarrassed and not worthy to be called a friend and a disciple of Jesus! I should have voiced my opinion to the Council that Jesus should not have been crucified! He was guilty of nothing! The entire trial was a sham and I said *nothing*! Here I am, a member of the Council, the Sanhedrin, and I said nothing! What a fool I am! Am I any better than Judas?"

Nicodemus approached Joseph, and at first simply looked at him, and then he stepped closer and wrapped his arms around Joseph and hugged him. I could tell their embrace was strong and then, they both broke into tears, and wept.

"I am just as guilty as you my dear friend." said Nicodemus. "I was so afraid the Council would reject me if they knew I was a follower of Jesus, so I would visit Jesus at night so no one would see me with him! Jesus taught me so many things about this life, and the next, and yet I was afraid to reveal this publicly. Like you, Joseph, I never said anything to the Council when they laid out their plans to have Jesus killed! I too am a fool and have betrayed Jesus."

Nicodemus then looked us both in the eyes and said "Come now Noam and Joseph, let us get busy. We need to spread this mixture of myrrh and aloe over the body of Jesus and then wrap him in these linen strips."

We were almost finished when we saw several Roman soldiers approaching us.

"Is this going to be where Jesus will be placed, in this tomb?" asked one of them.

Joseph replied to them instantly, rising and standing from the ledge we were working on. "Yes, this is the place sir. Is there something I can help you with?"

"No. Pilate sent us here to guard the tomb of Jesus. The Jewish leaders are afraid that the followers of Jesus will come here and steal his body, so they asked Pilate to guard his tomb."

Nicodemus then rose to his feet. "We are just about ready to place his body inside the tomb, would you help us roll the stone to cover it when we are done?"

"Yes sir. We would be happy to assist you."

When we finished wrapping Jesus in the strips of linen and carried him inside the tomb, we all knelt at the side of Jesus and Nicodemus led us in prayer.

"Now and forever my Lord, I will sing of your love and justice and I will lead a blameless life. As we come to you in prayer, please hear our words and do not hide your face from us. We are weak but look to you for strength that we can be your vessels and speak of your love. We pray that we can make sense of your words, that we will see you again, that we would have another chance to be your servants. May your journey to join Isaiah and God himself be short and wonderful. All praises to God Almighty. Amen!"

We all stood and left the crypt with soft hearts. Exhausted, both physically and mentally, Joseph called out to the soldiers and they helped us roll the stone to cover the tomb and secure it. The stone was actually quite heavy and it took all of us to roll it!

Then one of the soldiers went over to the secured stone and began stringing a cord across it. One of the other soldiers held the cord while the first soldier strung the cord to the other side of the stone and then each end of the cord was sealed with a mixture of clay and was imprinted with the stamp of the Governor.

"We were instructed to place this type of seal on the stone so we know there is *only* way out of it and that would be to actually rise from the dead. We will remain here on the outside guarding it to assure no one moves the stone. If Jesus is who he claims to be? We will certainly find out, won't we?"

Our work was done, so we gathered our things and began our walk back to Jerusalem.

"I was thinking Nicodemus, it is interesting that the Council is now fearful that the words of Jesus, you know, that he will rise again in three days, could be true! To place seals over the tomb and have it constantly guarded seems to scream of uncertainty to me."

"You are very wise, young man" Joseph said to me.

"Yes indeed" replied Nicodemus. Why don't you come with us to the synagogue? It will be a good way to end our day; in prayer.

When we arrived at the synagogue, it was very crowded and it appeared to me that the entire Council was also present. I saw the synagogue leaders, Talia's father, the Levites and the priests. Yes, they were all there alright!

The three of us sat and suddenly a quietness, a hush came over the room. There certainly was a distinct tension in the air when the priests saw Joseph was now in audience along with us.

Caiaphas stood and addressed the crowd. "Why are you here Joseph? You went to Pilate to claim the body of Jesus! He was not deserving of any respect and then you took his body away for burial! Jesus should be buried in the criminal's graveyard!"

Joseph then stood up in defiance and to address Caiaphas. "Why are YOU so angry Caiaphas? Because I asked Pilate for the body of Jesus!?" Joseph was now yelling, and his face was red with rage.

"Yes, Caiaphas, I did indeed ask for the body of Jesus! I want to treat Jesus with RESPECT, the respect he deserved. The respect that I should have given him publicly and not in fear of what people would think of me! I gave him clean linens to wrap his battered body with. I gave him spices as we would hope anyone would provide for us. I gave him MY unused vault so that he would have a proper burial, one of respect! And here YOU are questioning ME? You never treated Jesus with any respect! You never treated him properly and nor did you follow any of our laws with how you treated him under your false 'trial'. And even now, you appear to have no regret for killing this innocent man!"

The crowd erupted! They all stood in unison and began to tear at their cloth, and pointed at both of them shouting remarks so unintelligible I couldn't make sense of what they were screaming. Jairus took his walking stick and began to thump it on the floor yelling "silence, silence!"

Slowly, order came to the floor and Caiaphas told everyone to sit. Once calm was restored, he began: "You Joseph, have caused enough trouble and *your* accusations are blasphemous. Therefore, I call to this assembly to have this man arrested!"

The crowd erupted again and the guards came quickly and seized Joseph and took him away to a windowless cell within the synagogue.

Caiaphas remained standing while they took Joseph away. He said to all "The guards will put Joseph in one of our cells here, lock the door, place a seal on it, and have guards watching it until the sabbath is over. We will then convene as a Council to determine Joseph's fate for all of his actions."

That was it. Joseph, one of their own members and now he was an enemy to their power. Clearly, Joseph had finally stepped out and voiced what was truly in his heart and now he will be paying the price for that.

Talia
(Dew from God)

I am so thankful that Mary asked me to stay with them while they mourned and prayed over Jesus. They have welcomed me as their sister and I am grateful for this.

We left Golgotha and went to Martha's house to prepare a meal for the men whenever they would return. We also prepared spices to anoint Jesus' body after the Sabbath. It was just yet another way for us to express our love and respect for Jesus.

Mary, mother of James, looks at me with her soft eyes. "Talia, my dear child, come here and sit. You have done so much today and have seen way too much for someone of your age. Please, come sit here next to me."

I have to admit, I feel exhausted, both mentally and physically. Yet I feel comforted by these women. I feel their genuine love and compassion, and their caring hearts. Even in the midst of such sorrow, they are reaching out to comfort others. I believe this is what Jesus was showing us that we are to love one another just as we would love ourselves. Get out of self and be kind and compassionate to others.

"Mary, can I go with you after the sabbath to where Jesus is laid? I too would like to help with the spreading of the spices. I feel I am being called to be closer to Jesus, even though he is no longer here......like I am being called to his spirit. Does that make any sense?"

"Yes, my child. I believe that many feel the loss of Jesus and that we too can feel his spirit within us. I know what you speak of."

"We will travel to the tomb in just two more days", Mary went on, "and we will do our work together. Now go back to your parents and worship with them. Let's try to make this our best Passover ever."

Yes, it was time to see my parents. I needed to feel their love and feel the hope of tomorrow.

On my walk home, I thought about what my father had told me about several of the synagogue members, and they had wanted Jesus to perform some miracles for them in order to prove the authority he claimed to have. They never seemed to really even want to believe. Always testing him, asking for proof, always trying to "catch" him in some way.

My father said Jesus responded to those leaders like this: *"Only an evil, adulterous generation would demand a miraculous sign; but the only sign I will give them is the sign of the prophet Jonah. For as Jonah was in the belly of the great fish for three days and three nights, so will the Son of Man be in the heart of the earth for three days and three nights."*

I see the inn where we were staying just ahead of me yet I am still deep in thought about the meaning of Jesus' response. What a brilliant man he was. The things that he would say were always rich in thought. I suppose that was also very intimidating to those who were afraid of him. My thoughts however, bring me to the three-day periods Jesus mentions frequently. He would tear down the Temple and rebuild it in three days. Jonah was in the belly for three days. Joshua tells his people to hide for three days. In Judges, the girl's father detained --- for three days. In Samuel, the donkeys were lost for 3 days; Samuel stayed for 3 days; God asked David which penalty should He should impose – one of which was 3 days of pestilence in the land. In Kings, God told them to depart for three days. Nehemiah came to Jerusalem for three days. Ezra came to Jerusalem for three days. Why three days?

Just as I approached the front door of the inn, it was opened and there stood my father, Jairus.

"And *where* have you been young lady".

Jacob
(May God Protect)

I find myself at the synagogue to seek some fashion of peace within my soul. The sabbath is over now yet the streets are still filled with pilgrims and merchants. There is still a buzz in the air filled with energy. I can't describe it; it's just a strange feeling that all remains unsettled somehow.

"Jacob! My friend how are you? It seems like forever since I saw you last!"

It is Bartholomew whom is recognized as one of Jesus' disciples.

"Yes, yes, hello and shalom to you my dear friend! Come join me here. Sit! Please. Tell me what news you may have!"

In an almost whisper, Bartholomew leans to my ear and says to me "Jacob, come with me over to that corner. We will be secluded and out of ear-shot so others will not hear us. Come. Follow me."

I stood up from my seat and I followed Bartholomew to the corner he suggested and we sat together. It was an area, very dark in the shadows where we sat, almost unnoticeable.

Bartholomew leaned in towards me and in a very soft voice asked me "Have you heard the news, Jacob? Have you heard that the tomb is empty?"

"What? What did you say?"

"It is true my friend. It was Mary who first saw it. Then she ran away to get the others. The stone. The large stone that had covered the tomb had been rolled away! Jesus was gone! His burial linens were neatly folded and left inside but his body was gone! The guards saw it too! He is risen! I know it to be true Jacob!"

"But how? How could this have happened? That stone needed several strong men to move it. It was sealed by the soldiers and then guarded. Didn't the soldiers see any of this?"

"Yes, they did my friend. And they are afraid and left the tomb to report to Pilate what they saw. Pilate then reported to the Sanhedrin what the soldiers saw and now, later today, the Sanhedrin have called a meeting to hear of their account."

I felt as if I was in shock. I was having a difficult time comprehending while attempting to understand what Bartholomew was telling me. Risen? Was this what Jesus meant when he said he would rise in three days? My goodness, then that would mean He *is* the Christ! He is the Messiah! He is the Son of God!

"I have seen him, Jacob! I have seen the risen Jesus! The Christ Jesus, I saw him!"

"What do you mean? Where is he? Can I see him too?"

"You must listen to me Jacob. I spoke to Jesus! He came to *me* and we spoke."

If my chin wasn't on the floor by this revelation, it should have been! What does he mean 'he saw Jesus'?

Almost whispering, Bartholomew began to tell me how Jesus came to him and explained what he was doing while he was in the underworld.

"Jesus told me that he went down to Hades to bring up Adam and rescue him and all of the patriarchs. It was Adam, the first sinner, and all of his children is why he had to die on the cross. He said he was there to beat Satan and then secure him with unbreakable chains.

You see, Satan wanted a temple of his own, opposite that of Jesus'! He cast for men's souls baiting them with drunkenness, frivolity, slander, hypocrisy, indulgence, sexual immorality, adulterers and the like. He said that God gave Him the power to heal *every* sin and to enable men to bear divine things."

"Bartholomew, did this really happen to you? Were *you* drunk or delirious to have really *seen* Jesus and he told you all of this?" I asked.

"Jesus told me to tell only those who are faithful and to those who are strong in their faith. And then He said that He provides gifts to all that desire Him. It was then that He recited Psalm 18:46-49 'The Lord lives! Blessed be my Rock! Let the God of my salvation be exalted. It is God who avenges me, and subdues the people under me; He delivers me from my enemies. You also lift me up above those who rise against me; You have delivered me from the violent man. Therefore I will give thanks to You, O Lord, among the Gentiles, and sing praises to your name.'"

Bartholomew then looked at me with such seriousness and placed his hands on my shoulders. "All of this is true my brother. Jesus, God; He is alive and will live in the hearts of men for ever and ever. We must know this and tell all of those who want to believe to have the faith in their hearts to know Jesus will be with them every moment of their very existence!"

Suddenly, the leaders of the Temple arrived and began to assemble. Bartholomew and I are huddled together in our seat back in the darkened corner and in walks Nicodemus and a young man.

"I know who Nicodemus is Bartholomew, but who is that young man he's with?"

"That is Noam. From what I have heard, he helped Joseph and Nicodemus prepare and place Jesus in the tomb."

"Ssshhhh. They are about to begin."[10]

---

[10] This chapter is Interpretation of comments made from "*The Questions of Bartholomew*"

Noam
(Tenderness)

We were back again. Back to the synagogue after the sabbath. It was the day that Joseph would be sentenced for arranging the handling of Jesus' body.

As we approached the dais where they were assembled, I noticed they were all there. The synagogue leaders, the priests, the Levites, and Caiaphas.

Caiaphas watched us approach and pointed to the seats in which he wanted us to sit. We sat as directed and then Caiaphas called their assembly to order.

Nicodemus looked at me and said whispered into my ear "This will be a very interesting day my friend. Just wait and see."

"What's to happen with Joseph? Will the Sanhedrin kill yet another innocent man?"

"Patience dear Noam, patience."

In a loud, almost too loud of a voice Caiaphas, called out "Guards, go get Joseph of Arimathea from his cell."

We waited patiently for the guards to return. Time went on longer than it should have taken and then, finally, the guards appeared but without Joseph!

"What is the meaning of this?" blurted Caiaphas. "Where is Joseph?"

"Sir, he wasn't there. He was not in the room that we had sealed; he is gone! The door was still locked and the seal wasn't broken! We could not find him. And you sir, are the only one who had the key to that door."

Caiaphas was dumbstruck as was his assembly. They began to mumble amongst each other when Jairus said aloud "Joseph was one of us and he was a good friend of Jesus. How could he simply vanish into thin air?"

Jairus was just about to say something more when the guards who were assigned to watch the tomb of Jesus came forward.

"What are you doing here?" Caiaphas questioned. "You are supposed to be guarding the tomb!"

"We are here to provide you with our report sir. The tomb is empty!"

With that, the scribes, the Levites, the priests and all of the synagogue leaders stood and shouted, almost in unison, 'HOW'?! I looked at Nicodemus in just as much shock as the rest of the assembly.

"Silence! Everyone, silence!" Caiaphas yelled out. "Sit down and let us hear what the guards have to report! Silence!"

That subdued the crowd and they all took their seats once again. Caiaphas then directed the guards to give their report.

They began. "It was in the middle of the night. First there was a very loud rumble, like an earthquake. Maybe it was an earthquake, I'm not certain. The ground was shaking and then there was a great light that appeared at the entrance to the tomb! The light was so bright it was blinding and then something or someone appeared and rolled the stone away from the tomb entrance. Frankly, sir, we were terrified!"

The other guards nodded their heads in unison and it was clear to see from the look on their faces they truly had been terrified.

The guard continued with his report. "There were some women at the tomb when all of this happened and this person in the light was talking to them. I heard the person say 'Do not be afraid. Jesus is not here; He has risen, just as He said he would.' Then I heard him say 'Go now and tell his disciples that He has risen and He will meet with them in Galilee'.

Caiaphas then asked "Who were these women? Why didn't you arrest them?"

"We were scared to death! We didn't know who these women were. Heck, we didn't even know if we would survive from the earthquake never mind arrest someone!

Caiaphas said "I don't believe you."

The guard replied "You didn't believe Jesus either! All of the things he did to save people, cure them, heal them, and you still did not believe him when he said that He was the Son of Man! And now you locked up Joseph of Arimathea in a sealed escapeless room and you can't find him? Give me Joseph and I'll give you Jesus! He has risen, yes Jesus has risen and will be found in Galilee. As for Joseph, I believe that you will find him in his home!"

The chief priests gathered here were stunned and fearful. I could see it on their faces. Their plan to eliminate Jesus had somehow gone array and now there are witnesses to the fact that Jesus did in fact rise from the dead!

Caiaphas addressed the priests "We mustn't let this information out into the public! We will pay these guards off not to tell this story, but a *new* story. A story that the friends of Jesus ate the one's, his so-called disciples, who stole the body when the guards had fallen asleep."

So this was it. These power-hungry men who were afraid of Jesus and His effect upon *their* subjects, whom they had to make up stories about his blasphemies, slander him to Pilate in order that he would be crucified, and are now engaging in bribery to continue their lie. They are supposed to be speaking for God as priests and instead they are protecting themselves and their fiefdoms. They are the criminals!

"Come Noam, we must leave now" Nicodemus said to me. "I am heading to Galilee. I want to meet with the risen Christ Jesus!"

I looked at Nicodemus and simply replied "I am going with you."

Talia
(Dew from God)

The sabbath was over and a group of us left before daylight and began our walk to the tomb where Jesus lay. We were bringing spices to anoint Jesus' body. I was surprised to see that Joanna had decided to join us. She was after all married to Chuza who was the steward of King Herod Antipas and I wasn't certain she was a true follower of Jesus. Apparently, Jesus had climbed into her heart as well and was one of his followers inside the Temple.

Of course, Mary, the mother of Jesus was there as well as Mary's sister who was married to Clopas, and Salome who is married to Zebedee. We all made our way through the morning chill and walked silently speaking very little.

We were just about there when it happened! The ground began to shake violently, like an earthquake, and such loud noises that we couldn't hear ourselves screaming from fear! The ground shook so hard that we all fell down to the ground. When it finally subsided, we all stood and wiped ourselves free of the dust.

"Mary, what was that do you know"

"Talia, I think it was an earthquake. Is everyone ok? Is anyone hurt?"

We all were ok and began our last few strides to the tomb. What we all saw next took our breath away! It must have been an angel of some sort who was sitting atop the stone that had covered the tomb, except the stone had been rolled away! The angel was covered in a very bright light that hurt my eyes to look directly at him.

I looked towards where the guards had been stationed and they were all lying on the ground filled with fear, covering their heads.

The angel looked at us and said "Don't be afraid for Jesus is not here; He has risen from the dead. Come see for yourself."

I was afraid myself! The tomb was now open, the guards were laying on the ground shaking in fear, this *angel* or whatever it was, was awash in a brilliant light, and indeed the tomb was empty! The only thing in the tomb was the linen cloth that Joseph had wrapped him in!

The angel then spoke again. "Go and tell the disciples of Jesus what you have seen here tell them to travel to Galilee to meet the risen Jesus there."

Still awe struck and filled with fear, we all ran. We ran. My head was filled with uncertainty, and uncertainty as to *what* exactly was happening. How did Jesus escape from the tomb? That could only mean that he was alive, but how did he escape when that huge boulder covered his only exit?

When we all arrived to the place where the disciples were staying, we were out of breath and couldn't even speak right away. The men were looking at us wondering what we were up to.

Peter, one of the disciples asked "What is this all about? What has happened?"

I was amazed that they didn't believe our account of what had happened at the tomb! Mary Magdalene began to weep. "We have seen an angel, we saw the stone was moved away, we saw the tomb was empty, and we saw the linens that Jesus was wrapped in! Why don't you believe us? It is as Jesus has told us; that he would defeat death and rise to be with us again! You should believe! Our Lord has risen! Praise Him. Praise Him. Go meet him in Galilee! He is waiting for you there."

Petronius – The Centurion
(Unsophisticated)

"Qen, it is so good to see you again! Thank you for preparing this wonderful meal for me this evening! I am weary from the journey home and this tastes so good. Thank you, thank you!"

"Sir, you know it is my duty but I am honored and always pleased to make you happy."

"No more health issues then? You have been well since I left for Jerusalem?"

"Yes sir. My energy has returned and I feel at least 5 years younger!"

We both laughed at that. Yes indeed it felt so good to be back home again. The streets were filled with the usual excitement that the market and the merchants brought, and the smells of their cooking and fresh herbs and spices that filled the air.

After I was finished with my supper, I went over to the hearth to get closer to the fire where it was bright enough so I could read. When I was in Jerusalem, and witnessed Jesus up on that cross, a man whom I did not know approached me and handed me a scroll and told me to read it. It would help me on my journey he said. My journey? And then he was gone, blending back into the crowd.

The scroll must have come from one of the surrounding synagogues because it told the story of Malachi. I knew nothing of this man named Malachi nor his place in history, but I began to read it each evening before I retired to bed. I was almost finished reading it when I arrived here at home.

Malachi was the last prophet of the Jews and lived over 400 years ago. It is he who foretells that God will come to the earth and judge His people. He will bless those who have remained faithful and heal them, and restore them, fully.

He reminds the people that God will *fully* restore them when they ascend into His kingdom in heaven. It is God who has the power to restore all of us and all of our infirmities and scars and memories of our individual weaknesses. All of these things will be fully washed away. We will be fully restored when we are in our places in heaven! No more pain. No more scars. Just His love.

I have seen and learned so much during this trip. I know now that Jesus was more than a great man and it was through his suffering, and what happened while he was on that cross, that my heart was opened to something new within me. And then a risen-Jesus! He arose from the grave! Along with many others! Miraculous!

Jesus told everyone to have *faith* and to believe in him, the Son of Man. I saw it were those who were faithful were the ones who were filled with hope. They loved one another. They helped each other. It was a new community of brotherhood. However, not everyone felt the same way and many feared this new change in attitude and this new way would destroy the Law of Moses. In a sense, religious power was shifting away from a few and was being spread to many.

I saw it. I know too that it is human nature, built into us. Pride and power. It is a poison that corrupts and steers us away from the things that Jesus and God want us to do. I saw the priests, and Temple leaders, and even the Levites do the things that helped themselves, and not the people who came to them for help and mercy. They were no different than the people they were supposed to serve; they were weak too.

These Temple leaders, the priests, the scribes, all contributed to the fracturing of the people's faith in God! The people saw their corruption, and the way these rulers would create new laws to better suit their own needs and crooked desires. It was the same when I read Malachi. The people actually blamed God for not loving them and accused Him of not being there to help them in their daily lives. It was Malachi, an oracle of God, that told the people that God *was* with them and reminded the people of their own sins. Sins like how the Temple offerings that were being sold were actually crippled and diseased offerings. He reminded them of their false teachings, and of their hardened hearts.

Malachi lived over 400 years ago and yet these same things were happening right now! It is truly amazing. What has changed?

Jesus. That's what changed! I am seeing this so clearly. God sent His Son, Jesus! He came to save the sinners, He came to take away the sins of everyone, to heal us, love us, unite us. To love others as we love ourselves and to be faithful to Him, and be obedient to Him. He brings us salvation and the hope. Jesus was the sacrificial lamb! The perfect sacrifice for all of us!

He has changed me. He changed my life and I will be faithful and loyal to Him. He is in my heart and will forever guide me in my walk of faith. I saw him die on that cross and I saw him on the third day very much alive! This man was no man; He is God. It is His spirit that lives in me now and forever.

As I read the last chapter of Malachi, I closed my eyes and slowed my breath. My pulse was slow and a certain warmth filled my chest and body. I could feel the Holy Spirit envelope me and I was filled with peace. I knew exactly where I was going in the morning. I am going down to the river and I will be baptized in the name of our Lord. That is my future. Praise Jesus and to our Lord in heaven, now and forever, Amen!

Noam
(Tenderness)

We were almost to Galilee but decided to spend the evening at the home of Nicodemus. It would be much more comfortable sleeping in a warm house and a have a home cooked meal. And it was.

When we arrived, we were surprised to be greeted by Joseph of Arimathea! There he was, waiting for us. I supposed he saw our expressions on our faces and he began to laugh.

"You guys look as if you have seen a ghost." he says.

"Well, can you blame us, Joseph? The last time Noam and I saw you; you were being taken to the Temple prison cell! And then, after the sabbath, you had disappeared and no one knew where you were! You ARE a ghost!"

"Ha, well I suppose that is certainly true. I will tell my story tomorrow. Caiaphas sent me a message to my home and for me to meet he and some of the Temple leaders here at your house Nicodemus. They are very interested in where I went too!"

At this, we all began to laugh.

"Come, come everyone. I'm am sure Nadia has prepared us a nice meal for us to enjoy. Come, sit, eat."

That following morning we heard it. A knock on the door. It was a knock not of authority nor timidity but one of certainty. Since I was the youngest of the three of us, I stood and answered the door.

There stood Caiaphas, Jarius, and just a few others who were members of the Temple Sanhedrin. They were dressed, not in their Temple garb but items of less formality.

"Please gentlemen, please do come in and Good Morning to you all! " I said to them. I bowed slightly as they each passed me in the doorway. I really had no idea what they were here for. It was the last time that this group was together that they had Joseph arrested and wanted him to be killed.

Nicodemus directed them to the largest room in the house and directed them to their seats. Joseph was seated to the right of Nicodemus and looked calm as he nodded to each of the guests.

It was Nicodemus who spoke first.

"Good morning my friends. I trust your journey went well as you all look fresh. Nadia has prepared cakes and fresh juice here, so please help yourself."

Everyone was enjoying the hospitality and the mood in the room was definitely beginning to lighten up. I noticed Caiaphas shifting in his seat and leaning in towards Jairus whispering something into his ear. Jarius then tapped on the table to get everyone's attention.

"Excuse me gentlemen," he said, "I would like to call your attention to our Chief Priest Caiaphas as he would like to ask Joseph a few questions."

Wow. I definitely felt a shift in the room as everyone stiffened up and knew this was the time for the business at hand; whatever that was going to be. I did sense however, that Caiaphas did not have that arrogance that he usually had about him. He seemed almost humbled and less aggressive in his tone. Something was very different.

"Joseph, we would like to ask you a few questions regarding the events that have taken place involving all of us. We have brought with us the Scroll of the Law and first would like you to swear upon it, to tell us the truth, and answer all of our questions with absolute honesty." The members in their party all nodded their heads and looked towards Joseph.

"Of course I will take that oath." replied Joseph. "I too am amazed, and quite frankly am mystified by the events of this past week. I look forward to answering your questions as well as telling you the things that I have experienced. I have yet to tell anyone about this including my host Nicodemus and our friend here, Noam."

After the formality of Joseph taking the oath, Caiaphas began.

"Joseph. As a friend and a member of the Sanhedrin we were troubled for the things you did for Jesus. To go to Pilate and ask for the dead body of Jesus and then prepare him for burial and then to even provide a tomb for him to lay in. What happened to you that you did all of these things for a criminal of God and of the Temple?"

Caiaphas continued. "As you very well know, we had you imprisoned for these actions and locked you away until the sabbath was over. There was only one key to your cell which I had on my person the entire time and the cell door was sealed. When the guards went to get you, there was the unbroken seal, and my key was then used to unlock the door. When the guards opened the door, you were gone! Simply not there! How did you do this? How did you escape?"

All heads now turned towards Joseph. Joseph looked calm and he slowly took his time looking into each of our eyes. His hands were crossed and were laying on the table in front of us. He took in a deep breath and exhaled and began.

"I was praying in my cell, the night of the sabbath. While I was deep in prayer and meditation, all of a sudden, my cell block was picked up, like it was flying. All I could see was the room was filled with a blinding bright light. Of course, I was terrified! What was happening to me? In fear, I simply fell to the floor and covered my eyes from the light."

"It was then that I felt a hand grab my arm and actually lifted me back up to a standing position. Then I felt his other hand grab my other hand and he said 'Do not be afraid Joseph, it is me, Jesus.'"

By now the entire room was in a state of shock. We all were. Here was this man who had taken a Holy oath to tell nothing but the truth detailing his visit from the risen Jesus? He actually saw Jesus! Caiaphas raised his hands to his face as if he was in prayer. It was impossible to tell what he was thinking at this moment, but he was clearly shaken. Joseph went on.

"Of course, I thought this was a dream! How could Jesus be alive and be touching me physically when it was me who placed him inside that tomb wrapped in linens very much dead! How could this be? So I asked this Jesus, 'if it truly is you my friend, then show me where I placed you in the tomb.' And then he took me to the tomb! HE TOOK ME TO THE TOMB!"

Joseph was trembling now. Tears flowing down his face. He bowed his head onto the table and was sobbing. Then he said "And there we were, at the tomb, with the stone rolled away, and we both went inside. The linens I had wrapped Jesus in were laying there, neatly folded alongside the towel I had placed over his face. I looked into his face, and he smiled at me, and said 'It is me Joseph, I have done what I said I would do, I have defeated death so that you can live forever in My Kingdom!'

"After that he took me to my home and said 'Peace be upon you. I will see you in Galilee. ' And then he was gone. And as you all know, that is where your messenger found me and delivered your request to meet with you."

I looked again to everyone sitting here and everyone was stunned. Here it was. Jesus, the risen Jesus, had come to rescue Joseph from his captors, his accusers, and delivered him to safety. Reports have been rushing in that people are seeing Jesus and even those who have died years ago, have also risen from their graves!

I sat there in silence waiting for someone to say something, anything to break the silence. Most were looking down as if there was an answer on the floor or on the table top where they sat. Finally, it was Nicodemus who spoke.

"My brothers. We are all men of the Torah and faithful to the Law of Moses. We have witnessed so much that it is hard to comprehend. We have our differences with how we have interpreted the events surrounding Jesus and the things he has done, and I will confess that I believe that Jesus is the Christ; the Son of Man."

By now everyone was looking at Nicodemus and listening to his words. Even Caiaphas was looking and watching intently. Nicodemus continued.

"I am thinking of Korah, the son of Levi, a cousin of Moses and Aaron. Do you remember them Caiaphas? When they organized over 250 Israelites to oppose Moses and Aaron? It is chronicled in Numbers, Chapter 16. Korah had high duties at the tabernacle but wanted even more power and wanted to be a High Priest. Do you remember this Caiaphas? How about you Jarius? What about the rest of you? Do you know this that I speak of?"

Jarius spoke first. "Of course we do Nicodemus. It was Korah who was not satisfied with his position and wanted to replace Moses and Aaron. It was Korah who led the 250 council members to oppose Moses' leadership. It was Korah who accused Moses of 'going too far' and accused him of being above the Lord's assembly."

"Yes, it was Jarius. Those men lusted only for themselves and the power they thought they deserved. They were the ones who thought they were blessed by God to do His work." said Nicodemus. "Jesus came to us as a humble messenger, as the Son of Man, as a Redeemer to bring us the Good News. And the Temple, God's house, and it's leadership is responsible for putting our Savior to death for their own interests!"

At this, Caiaphas jumped to his feet and cried out "Blasphemy!"

Nicodemus quickly shouted back "No! No it's not; it's the truth! A new day is upon us and just as God destroyed those 250 rebels who were against His plan. And yet the people still grumbled about Moses' leadership so He had the other 14,700 inflicted with a plague who then also died. I believe that God will also destroy the Temple in Jerusalem in our lifetime Caiaphas! Like Korah and his followers, we have gone astray! It is God's power and His will that will guide us, not our own self-directed desires!"

Caiaphas, who was still standing, looked at his followers and said "Come, let us leave this place. We are not welcome here nor is Nicodemus welcome at the Temple. I don't know who Jesus is, or should I say, was? I don't believe any of these crazy, preposterous stories. It is all fiction!"

At that point, all of the leaders stood and followed Caiaphas out of the house.

What a morning! Miracles were occurring right in our midst and clearly some think it's magic tricks while others think it is the work of God. There are thousands now organizing small groups that are learning and encouraging each other in the Words of Jesus. It is very exciting and I want to be a part of it!

"Joseph and Nicodemus" I said. "It is time for me to go as well. I need to continue my journey onto Galilee and try to find the risen Lord, Jesus Christ. My heart is on fire and my desire is strong to find out more about how I can become part of this new way of worshipping God."

Nicodemus smiled and looked at me and replied "Yes, Noam I believe you need to go too. You are young and filled with energy and will likely serve our Lord very well. Go young man. Listen and learn and spread this Good News to all you encounter! These are indeed the most interesting times my brother. Go in peace."

Joseph looked at me and simply quoted from Isaiah 55:12. *"For you shall go out in joy, and be led forth in peace; the mountains and the hills before you shall break forth into singing, and all of the trees of the field shall clap their hands."*

I gathered my things and gave them both a hug and wished them well. I knew, in my heart, that I was to join up with this movement they are calling The Way.

How can anything bad come from being a loving body in the Name of Jesus? We all, everyone one of us, can carry the story and the message of Jesus Christ. He is risen and He will come again! In the meantime, we must be Christlike and be His ambassador and be His hands and His feet showing the world that there is only one God, and it is He who loves us!

Do you believe in Him?

Jacob
(May God Protect)

So much has happened and I am having a difficult time putting everything together! What I heard at the synagogue was unbelievable to me, and to the rest of us that were there. Bartholomew had told us that he had seen the risen Christ Jesus. The guards testified that they saw the tomb where Jesus lay was empty. Joseph's cell in the synagogue was also empty and it was verified that he was found inside his own home in Arimathea! How did he escape and how did he return to his own home?

The graves in the cemeteries were opened after the sabbath and Saints who were sleeping arose from their graves and they have been seen by family and friends throughout Jerusalem! Many say all of this is impossible but it *has* happened! It has happened as it did before in our history when Elisha rose from death not once but twice! So how can they say it is impossible then?

Those risen saints who were seen went into the Holy City and were celebrated by those who were there. Most everyone was terrified and Jerusalem was filled with unrest. I believe that is why the Christ Jesus told the women at his tomb that He would meet the disciples in Galilee. The believers needed to be kept safe and in unknown locations. The unbelievers, and there are many, are pursuing them and want now to kill them! This is all so crazy!

Tomorrow I will begin my journey back home to Nazareth. I have seen so much during this Passover and it will likely be my last as I am truly feeling my age. Even though my heart aches, I feel hope and now understand that Jesus truly has been sent by God. It gives me strength to know that the risen Jesus spoke to Peter first after His ascension. Peter, who publicly denied Jesus out of fear for his own life, saw the risen Jesus and understood that a loving, forgiving Jesus had indeed forgiven him. We all make mistakes and react to our own insecurities yet Jesus came to him and demonstrated His compassion for Peter and all of those who believe! The Son of Man loves us all in spite of ourselves and waits for us with His unending love without prejudice.

We all have been affected this week and we all have been given a new mission in our lives – it is our duty to tell this story of the Good News to everyone, especially to those who have never heard it! We have seen true power in Christ and in those who believed. His words, *"you have been healed because of your faith"* is so powerful and uplifting knowing that through Him we *can* cope in this troubled world. His strength that He gives to each of us and the comfort He delivers to our souls is powerful!

I now know that we are the Temple; His Temple. When we join hands and hearts, and approach people in faith and in love, show compassion, and help those in need no matter how large or small, it is then that we are His Temple. We accept others without judgment. We provide where help is needed. We are joyful when we are able to share. We are faithful when we are weak. We love everyone and even love the unloved. This is the Good News! We are here to fulfill God's purpose and we each have been assigned such accordingly to the talents we have been blessed with. And when we are done? We go home to the place where God has made for us and enjoy His everlasting love for all of eternity.

I now know, that even in my aging body, I have work to do to further this message and cannot stop until I no longer breathe the air of this earth. Father, my Lord, I am coming home and will be Your servant until the very end.

I finished my prayer, rose from my knees, and laid on my bed. Joy filled my heart because I was comforted by a peace I never fully felt before. But I felt it now. My heart was soft and my eyes were heavy, and I peacefully fell asleep.

Petronius – The Centurion (Unsophisticated)

"Qen, I have been ordered along with my men to deploy to Caesarea. Please assemble my things immediately."

"Yes, master. How long will you be gone, sir?"

"I am quite sure it will be a while. My commander has ordered two Centurions with two hundred soldiers, 70 horsemen and 200 spearmen to accompany a man who was named Saul of Tarsus to Caesarea. Now his name is Paul. Apparently, there is a plot to kill him and Governor Felix would like to meet with him in Caesarea."

"Ah, yes sir. Caesarea is a safe place as it is headquarters for Romans for this area. Indeed, he will be safe there for sure. Do you know what this Paul has done that he needed such protection?"

"Qen, these are interesting times for sure. Yet again, the Temple leadership is up in arms over Paul's actions and my commander has learned of a plot by some 40 Jews to have him killed. Caiaphas and Ananias of the Sanhedrin have once again gone after an innocent man and have charged Paul with being a ringleader of the Nazarene sect, a troublemaker, as well as charging him with desecrating the Temple. I am quite sure these charges bear no truth nor do they have any weight to them. Yet again Qen, these Temple leaders are worried about their own power and status that they will resort to any means to hold on to it."

I walked across the room and sat down at the table here in my house and began to reflect upon the things that have happened since Jesus was crucified and ascended. It truly has been amazing.

After Jesus rose from the dead, he was seen for the next 40 days up in the area of Galilee. I was told that He was with His disciples and teaching them more and more about the Kingdom of God. He spoke of the Holy Spirit and how the Holy Spirit would guide them, guide everyone who believed, to be His witness and to go out and invite everyone to live under His reign. They called this the Pentecost. People came from foreign lands, and spoke multiple languages but the Holy Spirit came upon them and suddenly they were one. One people. One language. One mission. To GO and make disciples of Jesus Christ throughout the world! And this they have called the Great Commission. Jesus has commissioned every believer to GO.

In response to His command, thousands of people have responded to this call and they have formed new communities of generosity while healing the sick and feeding the poor. It is amazing what they are doing and already have done in the name of Jesus Christ! They meet in their own homes, they meet in synagogues, and even in the Temple courts. It is infectious how their Spirit has generated such a following. They have begun calling it "The Way" while others are calling them "Christians"; followers of Jesus Christ, and His Way.

However, this is causing a lot of problems amongst the Jews! I cannot remember a time that they have been so divided amongst each other. The Temple leaders appear to be so threatened by these 'Christians' that they have resorted to violence in the hopes to break them apart and end this kind of crusade.

There was this one man, his name was Stephen. He was often found on the Temple grounds and in the various courtyards preaching the Good News of Jesus Christ. He spoke of loving one another, caring for one another, just as Jesus did. It was also amazing because Stephen actually was performing miracles and healing the sick, the same as did Jesus did and declaring that these miracles were from God Himself. He reminded the people that their salvation came from their faith in Jesus Christ.

And they loved it! They loved his messages of hope and salvation. And the crowds grew and grew to the point where they filled the Temple courtyards to a point where it was difficult to even move around!

The Temple leaders felt this as a threat. Stephen's messages and his popularity, and how his messages were being received, had him arrested. They brought him before the Temple council and charged him for being disrespectful to the Laws of Moses.

One of the Temple guards told me that Stephen fought back from these charges and told them how it was *them* who were disrespectful! Stephen walked them through their previous leaders like Abraham, Moses, Joshua, David, Solomon, all of them God's chosen and yet they all deviated from God's plan through the weakness of their own flesh and desires.

Stephen looked at the Council and then said "Why is it that you continue to reject God's messengers?" Of course, they erupted when he said this to them! They knew they had a problem with Stephen. Stephen looked at them again and said "You are the one's who killed the Son of Man, Jesus Christ, because you are stubborn and loathe anything or anyone who may be a threat to your own power! You are all poor in Spirit – spiritually proud and self-sufficient."

That was it. I am suspect it was the Council that spread the untrue rumors about Stephen and that enraged the people to a point where they began to stone him in the Temple courtyard. Yet it was another miracle that happened next! Stephen was there and then he wasn't! He was taken away! It was a Spirit or an Angel that lifted him up and away while he was bathed in white, a bright white, and then he was gone!

I was so deep in thought that I was startled when I heard Qen ask "Sir, may I get you something to drink? Water or tea maybe?"

"Oh Qen, you are such a good man. No, but please sit with me a minute. I'd like to tell you about this man Paul; the one we have been ordered to protect and bring to Caesarea. Please sit."

So I then told Qen everything I had heard or known about this man, Saul of Tarsus. Saul was a tent maker and he was trained in the Torah and was a brilliant scholar. He was very well respected amongst the Jews and its religious leadership. So much so he was appointed a Pharisee. Saul thought that Jesus was not who he said he was and this Christianity movement was a significant threat to the Jews. So he started his own campaign to kill all of these "Jesus believers".

"Petronius, I thought you said his name was Paul?"

"Well, it is now Qen. You see, the Spirit of Jesus came to Saul and asked him why he was persecuting His people and believers and then struck him blind. Jesus then instructed Saul to travel to meet this man named Ananias who would make him see again."

"Oh my gosh! And did he see again?"

"Yes, Ananias did cure Saul's blindness and then following the orders from Jesus, he renamed Saul to Paul. Paul was so shocked and amazed by this encounter with Jesus, he converted to Christianity. A man named Gamaliel, who was zealous for God and Jesus, then trained Paul according to the will and ways of Jesus."

Qen had such a look of amazement on his face and then asked "So why are these 40 men after Paul?"

"Well, it was Paul's nephew, Julias, who learned of a plot to kill Paul and he told our Commander. Apparently, one of the members of the Sanhedrin had been insulted by Paul and wanted retribution against him. I personally think that the Sanhedrin are very upset that Paul is now a Jewish Christian which is yet another huge problem for them."

"Sir, why are there so many troubles involving religion and people's belief?"

"Qen, I am quite positive that I do not have the answer to that question. However, I do know that we need to follow our heart, and what's in it. After all that I have seen and experienced, I do believe that Jesus is the Christ, He is the Messiah, He died on that cross, and yes, He did defeat death itself and rose from the dead! And I was baptized since that day and I also make claim to be a Christian, a follower and believer of Jesus Christ."

At that moment I found myself with tears in my eyes. Tears that humbled me and I felt the love of Jesus Christ surround me in that moment and I was overcome with a true sense of joy. Yes, Jesus loves me. I have this confidence too, that He is right beside me and will guide me in my actions and behavior if I only listen to Him.

"Qen, come with me and let's pack my things for my journey."

Actually, I am excited about this trip. I believe that I will have some time to speak to Paul and learn of the things he knows about Jesus and what Jesus has said to him. I have found that we should spend more time listening and even more time praying! There is joy in communing with Jesus in prayer – He has a lot to say!

Noam
(Tenderness)

"Talia, it is so good to see you! Thank you for putting the word out there as to where I could find you! I wasn't sure if you went back home or if you stayed in Galilee."

"Oh Noam. It is so good to see you again too! I have missed our talks and just being around you."

My heart was pounding. She looks as beautiful as ever; maybe even more! I have truly missed her and my heart feels like it's on fire. I'm not sure which is making me feel this way; my love for Talia or my fear of telling her I must leave soon.

"Noam, please tell me what you have been doing! The last time I saw you was at Jesus' empty tomb. Which wasn't that amazing? I mean, that Jesus wasn't there – "

We both giggled together. I knew what she meant and not that it was amazing to see each other there, even though that was true as well. This is very hard for me right now. I love everything about Talia! Her smile, her giggle, her sense of humor, her gentleness surrounded by her strength, and the way she looks at me and of course, the way she makes me feel.

"Talia, my life has been amazing since the day I was baptized. It has changed. My prayers have been answered. We both have seen and have witnessed so much I can hardly believe it! I happened to be there at the Pentecost when the Spirit came down upon us. I saw Jesus and was amazed when Thomas didn't believe that it really was Jesus. It was actually kind of funny when Thomas said he wouldn't be able to believe this was really Jesus unless he could put his finger in the wound. Can you imagine that, Talia? But Jesus let him and wow! Yes, it really was him!"

"My goodness, Noam. How exciting that all must have been!"

"Yes Talia. What about you? Tell me what you have been doing?"

"I have made so many new friends, passionate followers and believers of Jesus. I have recently been staying with Mary and Martha and their brother. We have spent hours discussing all of the teachings of Jesus and actually putting those words into action. Just like Jesus did and instructed us to do. 'Go' he said and that's what we have been doing."

I could tell that Talia was beginning to get excited as she stood up and walked the room, we were in. She continued.

"You know Noam, Jesus was often accused of being with those at the bottom of the cistern. Like they were the evil ones. The tax collectors – I mean who ever likes a tax collector? – prostitutes, lepers, social outcasts, those possessed with demons, troubled and sick people! Jesus turned their lives around when they believed in Him! When they had faith that He was with them. It completely altered our value system! No more animal sacrifices to atone for our sins – He died for us! He was our living sacrifice!

I now understand that it is us who are to draw strength from God in order so that we can give it to others. It is our own faith in Him that we can conquer any difficulty."

I am amazed by the things that Talia has learned and how she has matured in her thinking.

"Noam, Martha told me what Jesus had told her while her brother was dead. You know, before he brought Lazarus back from the grave. Jesus told her *"I am the resurrection and the life. He who believes in me will live, even though he dies; and whoever lives and believes in me will never die."*

"And then he asked Martha, *"Do you believe this?"* (John 11:25-26)

Martha's response to Jesus was her true confession – yes, she said and I know that it is you, the Son of God, the living Christ. I too believe that Jesus was our Messiah and I want others to know the story that the Son of Man came here to save us…..we just need to be faithful and truly believe in Him."

At that, Talia looked at me, smiled, and then sat alongside of me taking ahold of my hand and gave it a slight squeeze. My goodness, she is beautiful and her soul is even more beautiful! I cannot help but to believe that it was God who brought our two hearts together….and it is God who is directing me to leave her as I pursue my next mission.

"Talia, you are just beautiful and your spirit is very infectious. I love you so. But I must tell you what the Lord has asked me to do. He has filled my heart and is directing me to follow His great commission to GO. Go out and spread the Good News to those who haven't heard about Jesus and become His hands and His feet out in the world. I will be traveling with Paul as part of his team to help him set up new churches and develop new believers into strong Christians."

I now see the tears welling up in her eyes and her hands are shaking. My heart is breaking because I am torn in my feelings. I am confident that Jesus spoke to my heart and wants me to accompany Paul and somewhere along the way my mission will be revealed yet again. God will be molding me to do His works as He is always working in every circumstance and He will be using me to play a role in it all.

"Talia, maybe someday our paths will cross again. I will always love you to my core, but this is something I must do. I feel I have been led by my Lord Jesus Christ to follow Him in this way. I am truly sorry to leave you, and my heart is broken, but I know I must go. I must go and be a witness because it will be hard for the people who never met Jesus to accept Him. It is through actions and teaching His ways that we can build their faith about His love and an eternal life in His Kingdom."

"Go to the people and say, 'You will be ever hearing but never understanding; you will be ever seeing but never perceiving. For this people's hearts has become calloused; they hardly hear with their ears, and they have closed their eyes. Otherwise they might see with their eyes, hear with their ears, understand with their hearts and turn, and I would heal them.'" (Acts 28:26-27)

It is hard to be faithful in something you have not seen for yourself and that it why we are to be living examples of Jesus Christ. We are His messengers. We are His examples for others to see. Jesus is right there beside us. He will guide us. He will use us for His works. He will fill your life in ways you cannot imagine. We just need to believe in Him. Have faith in Him. To let Him hold us in the palm of His hand. Will you believe?

Talia
(Present day)

My life has been a good one. My husband and I have had four beautiful children and we have been blessed with 12 grandchildren and even now, 3 great grandchildren! Oh Father, You have blessed us indeed! How great Thou art!

The love of my life, my dear husband, left me here on this here on this earth only 4 years ago, which has seemed like an eternity to me! I miss him so and look forward to seeing him when I too arrive to our heavenly home. The time for me is close now, I can feel it within my soul. Jesus knows I have been a faithful servant and He knows I am tired. I believe that my work for Him is concluding and He will grant me passage to my real home, for I know he has created a space for my return.

I find it amazing that my name, Talia, has survived in our family for all of these centuries within our family tree. Of course, there have been gaps skipping a generation or two, maybe sometimes even three, but the name of Talia has survived since the days of Jesus! And even now, my oldest great granddaughter is named Talia! My granddaughter's family calls her "Tallie". She just turned 9. What a joy she is too. I am honored that she will carry on the family name Talia.

When I think of where we are in the world today, and the things that are happening, I simply cannot believe the patience that God has for us. We, as the human race, have not truly changed much at all have we? We suffer from this human condition filled with sin and tempted by so much evil that surrounds us and yet He waits for our surrender to Him. What a patient Father He is.

Like many, I often think that He will be returning soon, coming back to us in physical form, for judgment day. We read of the wars, and famines, and earthquakes, and floods and fires that are the precursors to the end of days as told in the Book of Revelation. Yet all of these things have happened for the last 2,000 years and Jesus still has not come. There are those who use this fact to deposit doubt into the hearts of believers and to the unchurched and cry out that there is no God! They claim that the Bible is just another piece of fictitious literature. I know you have heard it yourself. Maybe you too find yourself as a doubter?

And this is what I love about Jesus! He has told us that we must be *faithful*! I think of it this way. If I knew how my life would have played out, with all of the joys and celebrations, knowing that I would marry the one man that God led me to, have four wonderful children and three great grandchildren, lived (and struggled) in such a beautiful home as we did, would I have tried at all?

If I had known that I would lose a baby during pregnancy, that 2 of our children would suffer from breaking bones in an automobile accident, and another struggle with addiction causing strife within our family, would I have just given up and stopped trying to fix the problems we faced? We all need to have it in our lives; I needed to have it. It's called faith!

Of course, I had doubts in my life that Jesus was *real*! When I think of the people that Jesus met throughout His ministry, those He saved from sickness, and brought back to life and even *they* struggled to believe! The disciples who spent three years with Jesus, even **they** were uncertain as to *whom* Jesus was. Peter denying that he even *knew* Jesus in order to save his own life? They personally *knew* and talked and touched Jesus and they still doubted. "Doubting Thomas" had to have proof that it was the resurrected Jesus who stood in front of them at the Pentecost! Yes, we need to trust Jesus and be faithful, at all times, both in good times and in bad. Jesus has told us *"I am with you always."* I believe that He was and remains there has been right beside me throughout the years I have been on this planet. He has not forsaken me!

At times when I feel He has forgotten me, or when I feel unlovable, those are my thoughts, not His. When I have found myself in an impossible position and totally stressed out, I have found that it was ME who made those decisions to put me into that impossible position! Entirely MY choice. And then it was ME who expected that Jesus would make it all better. And IF He didn't? Well then, there was NO God at all! How childish we can be. How faithless we can be.

I now understand that the human race, God's creation, was lost in that moment at that tree in the Garden of Eden and it was redeemed at that Cross at Golgotha where His only Son died for us sinners, to save us all if we just believe in Him. It is our own pride and our own disobedience that destroys our relationship with a risen Lord! Yet He waits patiently for us, His arms wide open, waiting for us to come to Him.

Just then I hear a squeal coming from down the hall and a girl's voice calling out excitedly, "Gammie, Gammie, wait till you hear!"

And then she bursts into my room with her beautiful brown curly hair in pig-tails and ribbons, and says "Wait 'till you hear what happened to me today! You won't believe it, I know you won't!"

"Ok, ok sweetheart! What is it then? My goodness you're so excited! What is it Tallie?"

"Our church gave all of our Sunday School class their own Bibles today! Now I have my very own Bible!"

"How wonderful Tallie! Yes, that is exciting, isn't it?"

"Oh yes, it is Gammie! I've never had my very own Bible before and they told us we can even write notes in it and underline any of our favorite parts in Scripture."

"That is wonderful Tallie. That Bible is God's Word and He will teach you so many things that you marvel about for the rest of your life. You can always learn something when you read the Bible. It's almost like it speaks to you no matter what your circumstances are."

"And guess what else Gammie?"

"What is it sweetheart?"

"I met a new boy in my class. He is really cute and he has such a wonderful smile! There was just something special about him and the way he looked at me and the way I felt when we looked at each other."

"Oh, really Tallie." I said with a smile. And what is this boy's name?"

"It's a different name, but I like it. His name is Noam."